Oasis Reflection

Destiny and Desire Book One

by

Lola Valvet

This is a work of fiction. Names, characters, places, and incidents are either the product of the author's imagination or are used fictitiously, and any resemblance to actual persons living or dead, business establishments, events, or locales, is entirely coincidental.

Oasis Reflection

COPYRIGHT © 2021 by Lola Valvet

Contact Information: info@thewildrosepress.com

Cover Art by *Diana Carlile*

The Wild Rose Press, Inc.
PO Box 708
Adams Basin, NY 14410-0708

Visit us at www.thewildrosepress.com

Publishing History
First Edition, 2021
Print ISBN 978-1-5092-3669-5
Digital ISBN 978-1-5092-3670-1
Published in the United States of America

Her life seemed perfect...until it wasn't.

His subtle smile and the way he eyes her with desire make the decision easy about hooking up with him. *Fuck what happened with Alejandro. It was a fluke.* Besides, even the best-laid plans change sometimes. And end better than expected. Just maintain control around him—don't tell him anything. Use it for what it is. Just sex. She wishes she could think of a recent example of something ending better than expected but can't. There goes that negativity again.

When she returns, Parker doesn't hide the ogling of her cleavage, and his gaze rests on hers. "I'm not even going to ask you what took so long. Do you want to walk on the beach?"

"With a stranger? I don't know how safe that is," she teases.

"Well, we've pretty much shared life stories, so I expect it's safe. But what fun would it be without a little danger?" His eyes gleam.

I'm just going to go for it. What's the worst that could happen? I get laid, then enjoy the rest of my vacation sexually satisfied? I'll take that chance. There is just one rule. Don't get attached.

Dedication

To Chris—for letting me be me and you be you.

Acknowledgements

Chris, my awesome husband—He lets me dream, accepts my flaws, and celebrates my strengths. Thank you for unexpectedly walking into my life on that frigid November night, just when I'd given up hope.

My Family—Lisa, my twin, thank you for being my other half. Mom and Dad, I sincerely hope you never read this book. My face is ruddy just thinking about it. Thank you for always being my shining light. My bonus family—for their support and love. I hope they don't read it either.

My girlfriends—Thank you all for sharing your experiences, which was great fodder for the book. To Niki who beta read and gave me the confidence and feedback to continue. Roxane, keep sending those feathers—you promised, bitch!—to give me strength to do uncomfortable things. Cheers to us!

Judi Mobley and the team at TWRP—Judi helped me get this book to where it needed to be—those damn oxford commas. I thank my good fortune the day you got my first crappy manuscript. To Diana Carlile for designing the beautiful cover—makes me want to have an umbrella drink—and to everyone at TWRP who works in the background—thank you!

To you, the reader—Thank you for taking a chance on a new author. I hope you see a part of yourself in Amy and her friends. And whatever struggle you're dealing with now, I hope this book is soothing, so you know you're not alone, and reminds you happy endings are possible.

Chapter One
The Arrival

The whir of the plane engine wakes Amy. Bright lights pierce her eyes as the pilot announces the landing. She forgets where she is, at first, pissed to be woken from the dream about a hot guy licking her pussy while she sat on a cheap laminate countertop, her arms taking the fullness of her weight, pushing her hips into his tongue. *Fuck men. Who needs them?* She shoves her books into her backpack and dreads her least favorite part of flying.

She squeezes her eyes closed to avoid looking out the window at the world passing by so fast. The plane lands with a hard *thwap*.

Once at the gate, heads bob up and down, and people move so fucking slow while off-loading. *This is my least favorite part of flying. Be fucking ready when it's your turn for God's sake.* A tinge of jealousy rises from her stomach when a group of women, perhaps on a girl's trip, giggle and take their sweet-ass time gathering their things when their row is already streaming down the aisle. She isn't pissed that they take their time, she's pissed about being alone. Again. A couple in front of her struggles to get their bag from the overhead bin. When she sighs under her breath, glaring at them, her seatmate chuckles. She casts her eyes downward, guilty at her rudeness.

Outside of the musty, cramped space, her legs tingle. She takes in the salt air and citrus fruit—ah, the smell of relaxation. Or so she hopes. She surrenders to the gloriousness of a week on the beach, doing nothing. *This will be a perfect distraction from the freezing December at home and a shitty year.* Her mood shifts from the irritation at her fellow passengers. She reminds herself patience is a virtue—one she doesn't tend to have. Heat rises from the tarmac in the tropical sun.

The excited chatter of other vacationers spilling down the stairs into the concourse stirs anxious butterflies in her stomach—*I am going to be alone the entire week. What the fuck was I thinking booking this?* She has no choice but to follow her fellow passengers. *Oh well. I'm here now.* She surrenders to the idea of an entire week of relaxation, doing whatever she wishes.

At the hotel, she pulls out her printed hotel information and folds and unfolds it while waiting in line to check in. November seventeenth was the booking date. It was also the same day she traveled to the next town over in the dreary, darkened rain to sign divorce papers. It was also the day she got her last name back. Got herself back.

She makes her way to the mini suite on the eleventh floor and steps in, a smile stretching her lips. Ha. The twenty-dollar tip to the check-in agent worked. *I win.* The sun shines hot through the balcony slider, and the stained glass above it sends rainbow prisms dancing across the floor.

This will work perfectly. She forgets the irritation and hassle of a long travel day. A whiff of humidity hits her nose when she opens the large balcony doors. She kicks off her flip-flops, hops onto the king-size bed, and jumps, unable to wipe the grin off her face. *Just like Ava and I used to do as kids.* She takes her phone out to take a video selfie of her bed jumping to send to her sister. Her ex-husband used to give her a disgusted look when she engaged in this tradition and called her childish. She sees her grimace on the cell phone screen at the thought of her ex and tosses the phone down on the plush comforter cover.

After a few more bounces, she sits on the edge, biting her lip. *What now?* She glances at her small roller bag. The need to settle in—and organize everything—overshadows the draw of nicotine and the balcony.

She's careful to lay down a washcloth and line her low-maintenance toiletries and makeup on top of the fabric in the bathroom. She walks away and glances over her shoulder, chuckling at her neurosis and the perfect row of her toiletries.

Amy takes in her home for the week. She runs her hand over the rough wicker furniture, pausing to squeeze the silky-smooth palm tree cushions. She pauses to take in the photo above the bed. She admires the lazy way the woman is sitting on a dock, feet dangling, back to the camera. The woman's floppy hat covers her face, which is tilted sideways to the camera, making her appear childlike. *I wonder if the woman is smiling in the painting if I could see her full face. Probably frowning.* She shakes her head and grimaces. *Fuck your negativity.* She's no doubt smiling because she's on a fucking dock on the fucking ocean.

She examines the contents of the mini fridge and finds a Kalik, a local Bahamian beer. *I wish it were a*

Coors Light. She furrows her brow at her lack of culture, but her self-consciousness dissipates when she pops the beer open with her lighter and takes a sip. She grabs her cigarettes and cuddles, knees to her chest, into the overstuffed chair on the balcony. *Ahhhh. Yes, this is the life.* The sun heats her pale skin.

She inhales the first drag of her cigarette, sighing as the smoke fills her lungs, and holds the cigarette down low so no one can see. Not that they'd see it anyway—she's up way too high. A tinge of guilt follows the drag because this habit is well hidden at home. The therapist she saw once after losing Katy had told her, "Amy, you are too hard on yourself. You need to be kinder to yourself." *God. Why am I still fucking clinging on to that comment?* There it goes again. Negativity. After all that she's been through, though, who can blame her for being a tiny bit pessimistic?

The crystal blue swimming pool below calls to her. The distant waves crash on the miles of beach. People frolic in the pool, and two attractive guys spray each other with a water gun. She imagines herself sandwiched between them, their wet skin pressed to her naked body, caressing her—and each other—everywhere. No, she's here to rejuvenate herself after everything that's happened, not bang the first guy she sees and complicate her entire vacation like before. *It sure looks fucking tempting, though.* Palm trees and blooming tropical flowers line the maze of pathways around the resort. The floral air almost covers the smell of her cigarette.

She enjoys a few more beers and smokes. Her sweaty bare feet are like suction cups on the tile when she walks into the bathroom to freshen up. The long plane ride did little to help her long hair, now hanging in strings. The heat melted the dab of makeup she put on at three thirty this morning. Her grandmother used to say, "It's a magic world." Amy understands more of what she meant now. To wake up in one place and see the sunset more than a continent away is pretty fucking magical.

She dabs her sweaty chest with a washcloth and reapplies mascara and red lipstick. *Well, this is as good it gets.* She puts on a short red sundress that highlights her legs. A few years ago, around the time she turned forty, she gained a few extra pounds around the middle that refused to go away. She tries to ignore those and instead gazes at the deep V-neck and her ample cleavage spilling into the center of the dress. Try and be positive. That is the goal. Well, one of many goals.

Staring into the mirror and turning around, she gives the plumpness in her ass a little poke. She loves that song about men liking big butts. Katy and she and their other friends had danced to that hundreds of times, shaking their asses, making them proud of what they'd been given—even if it were larger than fashion magazine standards. Despite her shortcomings, her ass was never something she worried about, thanks to a boyfriend in eighth grade who told her he loved her bubble butt. At first offended, then proud, she was glad when that song came out so other women could shake theirs with abandon too.

Satisfied, she looked good enough to act confident at a bar alone—fake it till you make it—she sits on the bed in front of the mirror to make sure people can't tell she doesn't have underwear on. Her little secret. Men she's fucked think it's sexy, and the practice has stuck since her teenage years. *Not bad for a woman in her mid-forties.*

She ventures out to see the pool and the ocean up close.

Chapter Two
Daring Temptation

Wanting to hear the crashing waves and grab a drink—a tropical one with an umbrella in it—Amy heads to the hotel's thatch-roofed bar near the ocean.

People mingle and laugh in small explosions as they talk over the noise of the other patrons strolling past. A group of women about her age cackle over dozens of empty beer bottles. There's a group of men sitting together. They have empty shot glasses, a saltshaker, and lime wedges in front of them. She squints to read the insignia on their matching polo shirts but can't quite make it out. Amy makes eye contact with each of them as her stride takes her closer to that umbrella drink.

One of the men holds her gaze a bit too long. He's in his late thirties or maybe early forties, judging by the crinkle lines around his eyes and mouth. *Perfect age.* His biceps strain against his polo shirt. She imagines how they'd feel if she were grasping him while he fucked her. She shudders.

Tingles rush down her spine as his gaze roves over her body, down then up. The bright sparkle in his blue eyes deepen, his pupils dilate. Amy knows that look. She's sure her gaze reflects the lust coming off his.

Butterflies rise and flutter in her stomach; she holds eye contact as she moves through the lobby. *Is it my dress?* She knows it isn't and pushes her shoulders back, faking confidence.

When she's almost past their table, she makes a quick about-face and saunters toward them. Silence reigns. Their words and laughter hang in the air. She makes eye contact with the cutest one—the one that held her gaze just seconds ago. The one who sent a thrill of pleasure over her body.

"Do you know where the bar with the thatched roof is?" She glances at his crotch. Her face flushes. *I hope no one saw that.* She smiles at the man who appears to be the oldest in the group, maybe in his fifties. *He's cute too.* The flash of his ring finger shows he's off-limits. Amy shifts her gaze back to the guy in his late thirties, and he answers her.

"Yeah, you just go around the corner here and follow the path," he drawls in a Southern accent. "Need an escort?" They all chuckle and look away.

"I've got this, thank you." She nods, grins, and heads toward the path.

She can feel them gazing at her long after she turns the corner. She smirks when she's out of sight. *Fucking accents. Make me melt every time. Maybe I should try and fu— No, I'm here to focus on my relaxation,* she argues. She shakes her head to remove that thought from her mind. *No fucking or getting involved with anyone on this trip.*

She weaves her way to the beach bar, following the path lined, pausing to touch the delicate tropical flowers. The thatched roof hangs so low, she has to duck despite being just under five feet two. After the beers she had on her balcony, she licks her lips, ready for another cigarette and a drink. She takes a seat on a worn barstool, clasping the cool wooden bar top to pull herself onto the seat.

"Hi, Ms....?"

"Russo. Call me Amy, though."

"Amy it is, then. The bartender wipes the bar off with a towel. "Our special today is a Blue Hawaiian. Want one?"

She cocks her head to the side, trying to imagine what's in it. It sounds tropical and fruity and probably comes with an umbrella—a symbol of vacation. "Yes." *Fuck it. It's a year of new adventures, right?* Her spine tingles. New adventures this year. New adventures the rest of her life. It's about time.

The bartender places the drink in front of her. There's no umbrella. She rolls her eyes and takes a sip. *God, this is disgusting.* The sweet drink slides down her throat like the goldfish she swallowed on a dare in high school. *Ugh.*

"Do you like it?" The bartender asks.

"It's great." She lies and nibbles on her lower lip. She lights a cigarette and sucks on the straw, hoping the smoke will make the drink taste better. It doesn't.

She watches the bartender. He's cute in an older guy kind of way. He's perhaps in his early fifties but in good shape. His resort polo shows off his arms, teasing her with a partial glimpse of a tattoo on his ebony skin. The thought of his tattooed arms wrapped around her causes her cheeks to flush. *Nope,* she thinks. *Relaxation, relaxation, relaxation.* She should've brought a book down to distract her from all the good-looking men. The bartender turns and catches her staring. He smiles. There's a knowing look in his brown eyes, as if he's reading her mind, just like Kevin used to. The dream she had earlier on the plane causes an involuntary rush of warmth between her legs. And how can she forget the intensity of the gaze in Kevin's eyes when he slid into her?

Chapter Three
The Trailhead

Earlier that year, on an uncommon sweltering June day, she met Kevin. They planned to meet at an obscure bar between their two small towns. It took over an hour to choose what to wear—as it wasn't every day you planned to cheat on your husband. She had wanted to look sexy but not slutty. A fucking hard balance. Running the razor over her legs twice, she tried to remember the last time she'd shaved for her husband. She shook those thoughts from her head because her marriage had been long gone for years. She put on the finishing touch—red lipstick—and texted her husband to tell him she loved him and missed him. It was a big fat lie. She didn't miss him at all. She was more content when he was gone. He'd been away on a so-called business trip. Given the lack of sex, she wondered how much "business" he was doing. She suspected most had to do with his cock but couldn't be sure he was cheating on her. He didn't answer her right away, and her stomach dropped. What if he started texting her every five minutes? While she was on her so-called "date?" The anxiousness was short lived when he responded ten minutes later.

—*Hi, I'm super busy, let's talk tomorrow.*—

The butterflies dissipated for a minute and gave her time to take one last look in the mirror. *I look fuckable.*

The black eyeliner highlighted her blue eyes, which Katy had always told her was her best feature.

"You look mysterious with those eyes, yet like the girl next door. You should accentuate them with more black eyeliner." Katy was always good at giving a compliment yet "feedback" at the same time.

She waited in her black Mazda, twisting her hair around her finger. She knew it was him before he even pulled up. The whir of his motorcycle engine reminded her of bad boys and danger, which sent pulsing between her thighs. Anxious to see him in person for the first time, but not wanting to seem too eager, she looked for something in her car to grab so she'd appear busy. And not like the caged animal she believed she was.

Kevin climbed off the motorcycle, took off his helmet, his grin lopsided. His black-brown eyes caught the sunlight and twinkled. The tattoos on his arms peeked from beneath his tight Metallica T-shirt. Both of his ears were pierced, and his Levi's outlined the shape of his package. *The opposite of my dickhead businessman husband. He'll do perfectly.* She meets his gaze, and the door cracked open with a squeak.

He sauntered over to meet her. He hugged her, and his grip on the small of her back drifted lower than she expected, creating desire. When he released her, the scent of oak and pine drifted into her nose.

They walked into the bar, and the stale aroma of cigarettes lingered despite the smoke ban that had been in place for years. The despair of years past hit her nose like hope yet sadness all at once. It was a familiar smell.

Although they'd been emailing each other for weeks, her lips moved like a cartoon character as she told him about her job as a professor at the local university. *I'm not here to talk about my fucking job.* He had earned a GED while in jail and told her all about his addiction recovery plan—of which, so far, he was successful with. She knew all this already, having spent hours googling him and finding his many transgressions and run-ins with the law. It should have stopped her from meeting him at all. It was like one of her favorite movies from the 1980s, and she was a Soc, and he was a Greaser. Two different worlds. But in this case, the two were going to collide. They were going to rumble. But in a way she needed more than anything.

He didn't ask about her husband. She beamed at him, eyes grateful, as he droned on about his job sanitizing equipment at the apple packing plant.

While they talked, he glanced up and down her face and her body. Although not too obvious, his gaze lingered on her cleavage, which poked out from the black-and-green tank top she wore. It made her feel sexy to have him digest her body like that. She stared at his forearm tattoos, imagining holding onto his arms as he pushed himself inside her. She tingles at the high likelihood of that happening today.

Not really knowing how to start things, she blurted, "Do you want to go for a ride in my car?" *Wow, that was fucking forward.* Just as he said yes, she snatched the bill like a Humane Society dog that had been chosen after months of waiting. She paid and overtipped despite his protests.

"Let's get out of here." She led the way, feeling his eyes bore into her ass. Fake it till you make it, she kept telling herself, holding her head high and shoving down nausea and the flash of her husband's face in one of his rare moments of kindness.

He caught up to her and tried to grab her hand. *This isn't a fucking date.* The contents of her purse were interesting as she pretended to look for her keys. She didn't have to look. She always kept them in the same spot.

"Where do you want to go?" He glances sideways at her as they got into the car.

"I have a place in mind." She clutched the steering wheel hard to hide her shaking hands.

She was optimistic the trailhead in the mountains would be calming for her nerves. It was a place she went to often when she needed to be alone. Her visits there had increased in the last few months as her marriage went further and further down the shitter. She'd sit there, alone in her car, smoking cigarettes, trying to figure out how to get out of the despair. An answer never came. At least not a clear one. The only thing going well was work.

They pulled into the parking lot, and since it was a Tuesday night, there was no one else there. They both got out of the car and lit cigarettes. She chattered about stupid things to push down the nerves. He stared, acting interested, as she droned on about the black mama bear and babies she saw there once.

Let's just fucking get to it. The June air turned crisp, nearly like a fall day, as the sun set over the pine trees. Why isn't he making a fucking move? *I need to be needed.*

"So you told me via email your dick is pierced. Can I see it?" Fuck it. Be bold.

He chuckled. "You don't waste any time, do you?" The space between his eyes crinkled, and he unzipped his tight Levi's and lifted his concert shirt.

He took out his penis, and Amy's lungs expanded in one heaving breath. His flaccid dick must have been at least seven inches. The sight of a live penis, not in porn, caused the earlier guilt about her husband to fade like a YouTube video that was buffering.

He held his dick to show her the Prince Albert piercing, a barbell starting under the head and curving out over the tip.

"What do you think?" His eyes shifted to the ground, and he cleared his throat.

"I love it. Can I touch it?" *This is pretty much the weirdest come-on I've ever used.*

"Of course. What guy is going to say no when a sexy woman asks to touch his dick?" He laughed.

Sexy. He thinks I'm fucking sexy. God, when was the last time someone told me that? This gave her pleasure, and she pushed her shoulders back, feigning confidence. Finally.

She prayed the setting sun would make it difficult for him to spot her Jell-O legs. She reached down and put one hand around his dick to examine the piercing. His dick grew, and she took the full shaft in her hand, no longer pretending to look at the piercing. Electricity sparked from her fingers to her head. She wasn't sure if her trembling hands were from the cool night or the touching. Choosing to be positive, she assumed it must be because of the touching.

He slid a hand to the back of her neck and pulled her in for a kiss. His lips and the pulsing of his cock in her hand made every nerve shout, *it doesn't matter that you're married. Do it. You need this.* Warmth spread into her belly, and she leaned into him.

A delicious, needy kiss. It had been years since her husband kissed her like that. How odd it was that she didn't even remember how scrumptious those types of kisses were to her. She was sure Kevin would never withhold intimacy from her. At least not until they were a few years into marriage. She vowed right then and there never to get married again. That seemed to be when the trouble started. She released his dick from his pants and put her hand on the back of his neck, and his silky longish hair tickled the tips of her fingers. His lips were hot, and she was lost in his mouth.

His pulsating cock was rigid against her thigh. A stranger's dick brushing against her body was delicious and naughty.

She licked her lips and sighed into his mouth. She'd wanted him inside of her, now. She first whispered, then screamed in her head for him to fill her. Desire welled; guilt was pushed down. No, it wasn't a want. It was a fucking need.

She yanked at the button on his jeans, and they fell to his ankles. He continued to kiss her, harder, his tongue exploring her mouth and lips. He slid his hands under her skirt to reveal a panty-less ass.

"God, you're hot." He brushed his fingers over her swollen and throbbing clit. The word *hot* brought a surge of quivers that started from her spine to her head.

He moved away from the car, clenched her waist, and sat her on top of the hood. He spread her legs to reveal her waxed pussy, her skirt bunched around her hips.

"You have a gorgeous pussy."

Just stop talking and just shove your cock inside; patience is not one of her virtues.

He stroked his cock in front of her and raised his eyebrows. "Do you want it?"

"Oh yes, I do." Her body trembled. The intoxication of his hands on his dick and the impending thrill of what was about to happen made it difficult to hold herself.

In one swoop, he clutched her waist and pulled her toward him, pausing just to pull a condom out of his back pocket and slide it over his dick. It took a mere two seconds, which seemed to be two seconds too long. She craved him.

He grasped his cock and shoved all ten inches inside her. She gasped. The unfamiliar dick generated lust, making her hope this could become a regular thing between them. When you've been married so long, the comfort of the same dick becomes a habit. But the intensity of not knowing what is going to happen next caused her head to spin with giddiness. She was helpless and, inside, begged him to keep fucking her and never stop.

He slid in and out of her at a teasing pace while holding her at the waist. He moved his hips so every inch inside was like the fire that burned for a full month last July. It was a fire that continued to burn long into fall, and not even the first rain of the season put it out.

His strokes got needier, and he thrust hard and fast. She leaned on her elbows and gripped the hood for traction. She took in large breaths to accommodate for his eager thrusts. Being filled, being wanted, being fucked caused her heart to race and her mind to feel unsteady. He grabbed her wrists and held them hard down by her sides while she pawed the hood of the car.

He withdrew and slid her to the edge, startling her.

She raised an eyebrow. Instead of answering, he turned her around and thrust into her from behind. The force pitched her forward, and she grasped the sleek metal seeking leverage.

Oh my God, I fucking need this. His thrusts got faster. She was delirious, lust and need a tornado in her body.

The piercing rubbed her clit as he moved his ample cock in and out of her.

Without warning, he pulled out his dick and turned her around to face him. The pine trees whispered in the evening breeze, covering Amy's gasp from the quick removal of his cock. After kissing her, he muttered, "Let's get in the back seat. I want you to sit on my cock." She trembled in anticipation at the thought of sliding onto him and feeling his balls on her clit when she took him all the way into her.

She followed him into the car, pulling at her skirt, and the door slammed shut just as she climbed in. He patted his lap. For a second, anxiety filled her. *I'm out of fucking practice.*

Her deprived pussy clenched, needy, making that thought disappear. Her skirt slid to her waist as she straddled him, taking his full length in one swift motion. He moaned. She whimpered. Their intoxicated breaths intermingled, hot and heavy. She moved forward and backward on his dick, grinding it to be filled by his full length. She devoured his kisses like a hungry grizzly bear devours some salmon.

He pawed at her breasts, unclipping her bra, freeing her tits for his handling. He squeezed her nipples between his fingers, pushing her to the near brink of explosion. Amy slowed her ride to remove his sweat-soaked T-shirt.

Amy's panting quickened as his piercing brushed her clit every time the full length of his cock slid inside. Grinding, sweating, needing, carnal. Kevin moved his hands from her tits and put them on the headrest of the front seat for more leverage. His biceps pulsated with every push into her hole, she matched his pace, tilting her head back, taking large uptakes of breath. She wanted him even deeper inside of her, so she turned around, fumbling for a grip, to face away from him.

Her pussy dripped, desire pulsing in every inch of her body until she found his cock again and sat on it. She grabbed the back of the driver's seat and leaned forward, pressing her ass against his pelvis, so he filled her to her core. She lifted her weight up, down, up, down on his mammoth cock, exuberant to be full of him. Kevin reached around and found her clit and rubbed her bud, pressing his thumb on the top to match the intensity of the thrusting. Animalistic sounds came from both of their mouths, and she was thrilled he needed her as much as she needed him.

His piercing tickled her G-spot, and his clit-placed fingers made her entire body shake and spasm. She placed one hand on the condensation-covered window and one on his thigh. Her legs went numb and her head spun.

When she came, her scream and subsequent pants were intensified by his clit-rubbing, shivers pulsating throughout her body. Then everything went black. Her explosive release made the world feel as if it were crashing down, and all that mattered was the shivers vibrating throughout her body.

"Do you want me to come?"

"Yes, please," she implored, wanting to give him pleasure with her body. She slid on him fast, backward and forward, anticipating his release.

"I'm coming."

He moaned and mumbled, "Fuck yes," and freed his cum.

Amy turned to face him, his chub resting on her thigh and beginning to calm down after the release. The sweet aroma of sex, sweat, and pine trees filled her car. She was satisfied. Beyond satisfied. She took big gulps of air and collapsed, burying her face in his chest.

They shared a shy smile, and he glanced at her then looked away.

"Can we do that again soon?"

"Yes, please." She smiled as she pulled her loose bra around herself, brushing against the condensation that had gathered on the window. Her clenched handprint was still visible.

They shared a cigarette outside of the car, her hair sticking to her forehead, and both of them unable to wipe the grin from their face. She thought she'd remembered he'd said it'd been a long time since he'd been with a woman. She dropped him off at his motorcycle, and they both agreed they should meet again, soon.

On her way home, she twisted in her seat, skirt wet from his ejaculation and her orgasm. *Fuck, that was hot.* Tears welled in her eyes. She pulled over and switched on her emergency flashers. The red light on her dash incessantly flashed *blink, blink,* and the sound of the flashers covered the sounds of her sobs. Her chest heaved not from guilt, but relief. Relief from having to take care of her own needs with the vibrator.

Relief from feeling trapped. Relief from trying to make things work with her husband. She pounded the dashboard and screamed, "I need out. I need out. I need out."

She found a McDonald's napkin in her glove box and, heaving back sobs, dried her eyes. And vowed to change her destiny in her mundane, sad life, one where the only joy or pleasure came from work triumphs or time with her friends. There was no reason to live a life where your husband didn't want to touch you, where he was disgusted by you, maybe even repulsed by you.

Each time she and Kevin fucked; it was more satisfying than the last. He taught her what it was like to fuck against a wall, in an alley, tempting exhibitionism, in a motel room, dingy and quick, and on a kitchen counter, the smell of her spaghetti sauce bubbling. He schooled her on the best angle to bend to fuck in the shower, hands slippery on the wall. Although there were some twinges of guilt in part because of her Lutheran upbringing—having sex out of wedlock and cheating at the same time—she continued to fuck him. No one knew her secret—none of her friends and for sure not her husband. When she squirted all over Kevin's dick and soaked the floor in his musty apartment, it reminded her that before she was married, she had female ejaculations and orgasms with her partners all the time. Meanwhile, she planned her escape. Something about being fucked good kept her head clear to make sure her husband—or any man—never hurt her again. With Kevin, she'd promised not to be vulnerable. She'd succeeded. Like a cat homing in on a mouse, she waited and watched for the right time to leave her husband. That first cool June night she was with Kevin, as she pulled onto the road and drove, the darkness didn't seem so frightening. She just wished she were surer than she'd told herself.

****

"Miss? Miss?" The bartender waves his hand in front of her face.

She shakes her head to let go of the memory of Kevin and how she got here in this moment, in the Bahamas. The Bahamas. Oh, and that guy in the lobby. Damn. The way his hair fell over his forehead, and the mischievous twinkle in his eye when they exchanged glances. She can't contain the grin spreading over her lips. She imagines what it would be like to…

"Would you like another drink?"

Her cheeks flush from the thought she was about to have about that hot guy in the lobby.

"Yes. I'll have a beer this time, please."

Amy turns her back to the bartender to face the ocean and mumbles a thank you when she hears him set the beer down.

The ocean is uncharted and mysterious. She thinks she remembers something like eighty percent of the ocean remains unexplored. The mystery surrounding the ocean is only mystifying to humans. The ocean knows itself. It doesn't need humans to know it. The water doesn't stress about the weather. It knows the storms will come and go, giving way to sunsets, then span as far as the eye can see. It just takes time. Patience and understanding with oneself. This is something she needs to do but doesn't know how, not yet anyway.

The waves are like a trance that allows her to drink four more beers before asking for the check.

Amy pays the bill, tips the bartender twenty dollars. She's scooting off her chair when he looks at the tab.

"Umm, Miss? This is too much. Did you make a mistake?" He hands back the tab so she can correct the tip amount.

She pushes it toward him. "That wasn't a mistake. Thank you for the great service." After working her way through a master's degree and doctoral degree by serving in a bar, she tended to over tip.

She ducks under the thatched bar roof. The palm trees are fuzzy around the edges, not quite in focus—and not just because she refuses to wear her glasses. The warmth of the beers extends from her fingertips to her toes. She staggers. The air is silent except for the chirping of birds stuck in the open lobby. Are they happy to be stuck there? Or do they wish they were free like she had wished for the last few years? The low whispers of the hotel staff stop when she walks by. She smiles at them, hoping they don't notice she's tipsy.

Her sister, Ava, always says, "You were drunk last night? I couldn't even tell." Inevitably, Lexi, her wildest friend answered, "She's always in control, even with ten drinks in her." And all of her friends laughed, making her kinda proud. In control, always.

In the room, Amy leaves her clothes in a pile and climbs into bed. Naked sleeping is a new thing—and she can't imagine why she went along with her ex-husband's perspective that it was "gross." Sleeping naked makes her feel sexier. She reaches down and puts a finger into her own wetness and rubs herself in slow circles. The earlier thoughts of the faceless man on the plane disappear—as she imagines being bent over for that guy she talked with earlier in the lobby. His biceps bulge. His strong, workers hands would hold her by the waist as he pounds into her. She's impatient, and with every imaginary penetration, she inhales a deep breath, twitching and needing the release. The world falls to black; she pants and lets out a tiny cry, and the orgasm sends shivers throughout her body like ocean waves crashing. Just what she needed to fall into a deep, alcohol-induced sleep.

Chapter Four
Pool Day

Amy squints through the sun coming into her room to see the clock. *Nine. Nice. Big difference from my normal five-thirty a.m. wake-up.*

Despite being well rested, she longs for the warmth of caffeine to soothe her throat. Too many cigarettes last night. Pulling herself up and putting her weight on her elbows, she searches the room for options. She frowns at the small four-cup coffee maker and powdered cream on top of the dresser. *Fucking powdered cream. I deserve better than that.* Her thoughts about what she deserves have changed due to recent events. She picks up the phone from the nightstand and orders a basket of sweet rolls and a pot of coffee with real cream from room service.

The morning December sun draws her to the balcony. Her mouth drops at the beer bottles and cigarette butts spread throughout the balcony from last night. She bends over to pick them up, and there's a burn hole in one of the plush chair cushions. *Shit, I hope I didn't do that. Maybe I was drunker than I thought.* The palm tree print curtains sway in the ocean breeze while she sits on the balcony. The curtains remind her of her parents' house. They've been married for forty years, and it's apparent they still love each other. Although she's sure they've had problems, he still slaps her ass when he passes her in the kitchen. She and her sister, Ava, exchange disgusted looks when this happens, but deep down, they both think it's cute.

Amy jumps when she hears a knock at the door. Room service? That was quick. The server is a cute young surfer-looking guy. She resists the urge to smooth the loose strands that have fallen out of his ponytail. *I'd fuck him.* She reaches for the check and doesn't pull her robe together when it falls apart over the top of her breasts. Not sure if he's smiling from the display or the over-tipping, she purses her lips together and waves goodbye to him. *I wonder if he'd want to give me a tip.* She chuckles at her stupid pun and weaves out to the balcony to people watch and drink her coffee. She cranes her neck to see if those two hot guys are out there again today. The coffee is more tan than brown due to all of the creamer. Her ex-husband always looked disgusted at the large amount of creamer she used, pointing out how many calories she was drinking. *Asshole.* She pours more creamer in to make a point—to whom, she doesn't know. Maybe herself.

Amy doesn't spot the two men but focused her attention on a couple sitting sideways on their lounge chairs facing each other. She fumbles in her backpack for her glasses so she can see them better. He leans in close, his eyes cold. She wonders who's at fault for the assumed argument. He points a finger at the woman, and her gaze looks past him as if this is just one of the hundreds of times he's been mad. He's doing most of the talking. The woman rubs her neck. Amy sets her coffee down and leans in and watches them, then averts her gaze at their private moment, feeling a bit guilty. She glances at them once more before vowing not to overthink their drama. *Their fight is all too familiar.* Irritated for looking and annoyed at the knot in her stomach, she averts her eyes to focus on someone else. That part of her life is over. Thank God.

The giggles of two small children as their mother tosses them into the pool float to Amy's balcony. She bites her lip. Was it a mistake to decide not to have children? *Nah, it was the right choice to not have kids with that asshole.*

The coffee tastes even hotter on the balcony, the sun's heat already radiating from the tiled floor. It's a perfect day for drinking and reading by the pool. Amy finishes her coffee and basket of sweet rolls in between smoking cigarettes, then heads inside to change.

She pulls out one of the three swimsuits she brought, a short-skirted bikini, and frowns at it. With a little bit of struggle, she tugs on the solid black bottoms and fondles the mesh around the skirt, meant to hide her thighs. Fucking swimsuits. After pulling on the yellow-and-black polka dot top, she packs her beach bag, avoiding her reflection in the mirror the whole time. Sunglasses, check. Towel card. Check. Kindle. No. Real book. Check. Chapstick. Check.

Her mood changes at the idea of a pool, and she forgets about the sweat still on her upper lip from trying to get the swimsuit on—an issue that feels constant over the years no matter what size she is. Her chest is light, and she has a hard time wiping a grin from her face as she walks down to the pool and thinks about a conversation she had with one of her best friends before she left.

"What are you going to do all day by yourself?" Emma took a sip of wine, peering at Amy over the glass.

"Sit by the pool, have drinks, you know, the same things we did when we were in Cabo San Lucas together." Amy acted confident about her decision to travel alone and pushed down the lump in her stomach.

"All alone, though? Granted, I know you're independent now and all, but that just doesn't sound like much fun."

"It will be." Amy pushed her shoulders and straightened her spine. "I'll have time to read, people watch, and choose my own schedule."

"Well, I guess so. But a week is a long time to be alone."

Amy changed the subject after that because there were few things better than a week doing whatever she wanted. Finally.

Excited to be near the beach and have the convenience of ordering drinks from her lounge chair, she settles into a spot next to the pool but away from splashing children. Chlorine fills the air, stinging her nostrils. People's voices at the bar boom over one another to be heard.

Perfect spot. Fuck, I forgot sunscreen. Yes, Kate, I fucking hear ya.

Katy, her best friend, died last year at forty-one from skin cancer, and Amy hears her voice in her head every time she goes out into the sun. She slips her flip-flops on and makes her way to the lobby, the key card tucked between her already sweaty breasts.

She presses the button for level eleven and waits as the molasses-like elevator makes its way to her floor. When the doors open, she jumps out. She sees his biceps first. And a broad chest. She glances up. It's just floor nine. She forces a giggle and steps back in, irritated with herself for acting like every person does when the elevator stops at an unexpected floor. She looks into the face of the guy she got off to last night. Part of the group she asked for unneeded directions.

"This is going up."

"Yeah, I'd like to be going down," he drawls, smirking and looking her up and down, his gaze fixed a bit too long on the key card between her boobs. *His accent? Tennessee? Kentucky?*

"Mmm, then perhaps you should wait for the next one?" She stares at the floor-number buttons.

He steps on anyway, and Amy reads the logo on his polo shirt that she wasn't able to make out the night before.

"Thompson Elevator Company?"

"Yeah, I'm down from the United States, and my team and I are working on the installation of elevators at the new resort next door." He raises his chin to look at her.

"Oh." *Clever fucking response.*

The elevator reaches her level, and she gets off and looks over her shoulder. "Have a wonderful day." This is her typical energetic and upbeat response to just about everyone.

He holds open the elevator door, and his thick flexed arms catch her eye. "Hey, what are you doing later? Want to meet for a drink? I'm off at six."

"Maybe. I don't know what my plans are." She switches her gaze from his face to his biceps, trying to act nonchalant. *God, he's fucking forward.* Heat floods her cheeks, remembering Kevin's similar forwardness and taking control during sex. *Fucking hot.*

"See you at the thatched-roofed beach bar tonight, then?" He draws out the word "then." Damn sexy accent.

"Yeah, maybe." Just as the elevator beeps, he moves his arm to let the doors close.

Barely audible, he says, "So that's a yes." She isn't sure if he's saying it to her or himself.

Amy scurries into her room, distracted and forgetting for a second why she came here. *Right. Sunscreen. For you, Katy.* She goes to the washcloth and plucks the sunscreen from the perfect lined row of toiletries. Her body lotion had fallen over, and she set it upright, satisfied. She reaches into her swimsuit top, rubbing the lotion in, spending a little more time than necessary on the tops of her breasts. When she's done, she heads to the pool, trying to push the elevator incident out of her mind. After all, she's here for herself, not to have drinks with some guy. Although she'd love to get laid. And as she learned with Kevin, she doesn't have to be emotionally involved. Vulnerable. Vulnerable like with her ex. *Nope, I'm here to reconnect with myself and my needs. To think about everything that's happened—breaking things off with Kevin, divorce, and Katy.* But maybe sexual needs are needs? Maybe it can just be sex and nothing more, like with Kevin? Arriving at her chair, she orders a mimosa to push those thoughts away.

The day is perfect and flawless. The five mimosas cause her lips to tingle and her head to spin. Unable to read her book, she decides to walk on the beach to feel the sand between her toes.

Chapter Five
Unexpected Gift

She holds her arms out to the side to gain balance while putting on her flip-flops and looks around. No one will bother this stuff. The champagne bubbles in her head, walking down the stairs, and she grasps the handrail. Stairs divide the resort from the beach, and people bombard her, selling everything from hair braiding and bags to sun hats. She smiles and shakes her head to each of them as if the smile makes up for not buying something. She kicks her flip-flops off, and they land on the sand, so she can tiptoe, barefoot, toward the ocean. The sun warms her skin, and the incoming waves cool her feet. She shivers thinking about the cold at home. The sounds of children playing in the water, seabirds, and waves crashing. *This is fucking heaven. I wonder if they have teaching jobs down here.* Just the ability to think about moving to a different location sends tingles—not from the champagne this time—down her spine, in a good way.

Two dogs chase each other on the edge of the water in the distance, their play barks silent but obvious from a distance. As she strolls, she watches them chase each other. *I miss Casey.* She let her ex-husband have her dog in the divorce because the condo she bought wasn't ideal for her dog. Not enough space. *Besides, I was traveling every weekend to help Katy when she was so sick.* Despite the justification, a tinge of sadness hits her belly.

When she steps onto the hotel stairs, the top of her flip-flop catches on a tread, and she face-plants onto the concrete. She checks for blood and finds none, disappointed because the stinging radiates throughout her leg. She can't help but laugh thinking what Katy would have said. "They're all going to laugh at you." Kinda teasing her and referencing one of their favorite 1970s horror movies. Katy knew her so well. She knew of her fear of failure. Of looking stupid. All the while, appearing in complete control. Of everything. Confident. The physical pain of the fall is easy to forget. The pain of wanting to talk to Katy one more time isn't.

She returns to her chair and finds a note along with a small crossbody bag, the same kind sold on the beach. Puzzled, and sure it's a mistake, she picks up the note and reads the block letter writing. "Use this for your room key instead of your breasts. They're too stunning for that."

What the fuck? She looks around to who it might've been. *Weirdo. Who'd leave this for me?* She inspects the bag and fondles the embroidered, bright yellow-and-black design, and smiles. It matches her swimsuit. She puts her room key in it, along with her phone, rubbing the embroidered design one more time before putting it in her beach bag. Wanting to obsess about it, she chooses not to. She leans the chair on the flattest setting and closes her eyes, letting the sweet peace of sleep take over.

She wakes a couple of hours later, gathers her things, turns in her towel, and eats a late lunch at the buffet. She shovels in all the unhealthy food she tries not to allow herself at home—French fries, fettuccini Alfredo, and for dessert, chocolate mousse. *This is why you're thick in the middle. Fuck it.* There's control over everything else in her life, but eating isn't one of them. She takes the last bite of mousse.

On the walk to her room, her body feels weighed down from all the food, the sun, and champagne. Her palms are damp, and she uses them to wipe the sweat that has gathered on her upper lip. It isn't all because of the Bahamas heat. Some of it is anxiety because she knows she needs to check her work email. Well, she doesn't *have* to, but she hates feeling behind on work. *You are on fucking vacation. Let it go, let it go.* But she can't. Leaving her swimsuit on, she responds to emails and organizes a to-do list for when she gets home. Always in control. Well, almost always, except for Katy's illness and her ex-husband's behavior toward her.

"Always with the lists." Katy loved poking fun at her organization and control over every aspect of her life.

"It makes me good at my job—teaching one hundred plus students a term and balancing research and other bullshit work stuff I have to do." That was Amy's rationale.

To which Katy always responded, "A girl's gotta have a little fun once in a while." And Amy would ignore her, complete the list, and feel better with each item she added, and eventually crossed off.

She slams her laptop shut and grabs a cold beer from the back of the fridge and settles on the balcony. The palm trees sway in the breeze, and shadows begin to cast on the pool, causing people to pack their things and leave.

Is the bag from the elevator guy? It must be. Who else would it be from? *I'll go down and meet him. No, I shouldn't. I'm here to focus on myself.* One drink won't hurt. She considers the way he smirked at her and the way his eyes crinkled. *Oh God, and that accent. Maybe I should just fuck him once, then focus on myself and my vacation. Nope. Remember the last time you had vacation sex? And how that turned out?* Her heart had gotten too involved. Told him too much. Shaking her head, Amy picks up her book and begins reading while enjoying chain-smoking and too many beers.

A familiar ache, like a brick in her stomach, creeps in as she reads. The book is about two best friends and their life from childhood to adulthood together. They were there for each other through everything. She tastes the salty tears, irritated she lets them slide down her face. *Katy and I will never have that.* Anger wells. It's bullshit. Granted, Katy had been in pain for a long time, and maybe it was better she died, but fuck. Missing her is an ache that just doesn't seem to go away.

Fuck this. There's no crying on vacation. She stumbles through the slider to get changed, leaving a handprint on the glass. *I shouldn't have drunk that last beer.*

Amy peers in the closet for something to wear. *Something that says I'm not trying too hard.* She shifts her weight back and forth, reviewing the options, and decides on a short, sleeveless yellow dress, the deep V-neck settling in between the middle of her breasts. She rifles through the drawers looking for a push-up bra. *Who needs a push-up? You're here to relax by yourself.*

Despite the self-pep talk, she finds the bra, puts it on, and pulls her breasts from the side to create more cleavage.

I'll walk to the beach bar, and it's not because of him. I just want to be close to the ocean and chase away memories created by this stupid book. Maybe he won't be there, anyway.

Chapter Six
You're Late

She stumbles to the bar, ducking needlessly again when she enters. Pop music plays a bit too loud. A song she doesn't recognize. All the patrons are talking over the music, and their laughing booms. Amy peers at them, wistful. She misses her friends. She puts on a brave face and straightens her stride. *Being alone is a new thing, but I've got this.* She picks the same barstool from last night, and when she pulls it out, it's sticky underneath. She wipes her hands on her dress.

She orders a beer from the same bartender as last night. *His eyes are kind.*

Her beer is halfway gone when she hears, "you're late," from behind her. The drawl of his voice is unmistakable.

Butterflies invade her stomach. It's elevator guy. *Fuck him. I never agreed to meet him, so I am anything but late.*

"I'd be late if I'd committed to having a drink with you." She raises her eyebrows. "But I didn't, so I'm not late." Proud of the way she didn't let him tell her what to do, she sits straight on the barstool and regains control.

"Oh, come on. You know you wanted to meet me." His grin is mischievous. He takes the seat next to her, uninvited. He's wearing a black T-shirt that reads, "if it ain't country it ain't music." *Fucking cute.*

Amy can't decide if his cockiness is sexy or annoying. Given the drinks she's had today, she decides it is more sexy than not. So she teases him with her own version of self-confidence.

"I'm just a girl who uses her boobs as a room key holder and who jumps off the elevator as soon as the doors open. I'm also a girl who doesn't like surprise gifts from creepy guys." The edges of her lips raise into a sly smile.

"Oh yeah? What about gifts from non-creepy guys?"

"No different." She chuckles. "But thank you." *So he's the one that left that note. Screw him for being so charming.* She swivels in her stool to face him, careful to avoid the sticky underpart of the stool.

"How was the elevator installation business today?"

"It was good. We're close to finishing the installation and will be able to fly home in a few days."

"Where's home?" She reaches for her ring finger, a nervous habit she hasn't quite been able to give up. She's grateful, for the thousandth time, it's empty.

"Just outside Nashville, Tennessee. What about you?"

"Washington State." This is the kind of small talk she avoids. *I get enough of this bullshit at work.*

She either wants him to go away or engage in a deeper conversation. She swallows hard and questions with a downcast gaze, "So what would your wife think about you sitting here talking with me?"

"I'm divorced."

"So am I. It was for the best. How long have you

been divorced?" She runs her sentences together like a five-year old when they ask too many questions.

"Almost two years. The worst part about it is not seeing my four-year-old daughter as often as I'd like. I miss her."

Now we're talking. Small talk—no thank you. Deeper conversations—yes.

"Why did you get divorced?" He raises his eyebrows at Amy.

"I was young when I got married. He checked all the boxes—excellent job, good education, and comes from a good family. We helped each other a lot in the beginning with our careers, but as I got older, I realized there needed to be more to keep the fire burning. Besides, it got to a point where it was all about him. I think he was always selfish, but I didn't realize it until later. When I pushed back on that, we started fighting all the time. Plus, we never had sex, and sex is important," she says without taking a breath, searching his face for a reaction, and not sure why she's giving him so many details.

"For sure. What made you end it?" *Very perceptive.*

"He didn't like the strong woman I was becoming when I finished my PhD and earned tenure at my university." She sits taller and straightens.

"I like powerful women. Particularly strong ones who can help me load the boat to go fishing, ones that can help move the couch, you know, stuff like that."

"Whatever." She laughs. "You know what I mean." *Damn, he's adorable.* Try not to like him too much.

"I do. But enough about that. You're on vacation, and no need to think about an unpleasant past." He reaches his hand to touch her knee. Although his hands are clean, the grease under his nails is still visible. *A working man. I like those.*

"The whole marriage wasn't unpleasant, but became that way."

"Yeah, same here. Everything changed when we had our daughter."

"I can see that. Although my ex and I didn't have kids, I know it changed a lot of things for my friends who did, for better or worse, depending on the relationship."

"True that." He gets the attention of the bartender, giving her the opportunity to study his profile.

The extra he carries around the middle is more obvious than it was in his work polo shirt. Amy's heart flutters when his eyes crinkle right before he's about to say something funny. She wants to brush the hair that has fallen over his forehead to the side. *Resist, resist, resist. Remember Cabo San Lucas. You promised yourself. That was the last time you'd be vulnerable to any man.*

They order several more drinks and talk about everything. His constant travel installing elevators seemed to have a negative impact on his marriage. Considering the impact her ex-husband's travel had on their marriage, she wonders if it's because he cheated.

Before she can raise her eyebrows in his direction and inquire, he looks long and hard at her, as if reading her mind, "I was always faithful to her." They talk about her job, and she gives him the CliffsNotes version about what she does as a professor.

"How do those students focus in class with you?"

Damn your crinkling eyes. Leaving out the nights

alone, scrolling through her TV for a stupid Netflix show to watch, and the eight months helping taking care of Katy during every spare moment, she gives him the abridged version of her life. *No one wants to hear fucking drama.* Plus, the intensity of the emotions around Katy is too strong to share with a stranger. Fuck, she didn't even share those emotions with her friends.

"Are you dating anyone at home?"

"No, nothing serious. The town I live in is too small for dating. My biggest nightmare is posting my profile on a dating site and having one of my students answer."

"Yeah, that'd be pretty awkward." He shakes his head in agreement, his mouth turning up at the corners.

He ordered more drinks. They agree on how hard dating is when you're older. He recanted some of his dating war stories, and she heaved deep breaths in between bouts of laughter. He couldn't help but join in, tears of laugher spilling in the corners of their eyes. He brushed his hand several times over hers to make a point about something he was talking about, causing electricity between their two hands. She checks her phone, a nervous habit, and can't believe the time has gone so fast with him. She exclaims, "Oh my gosh! I don't even know your name. What is it?"

"It's Parker Allen," he responds. "What's yours?"

"Amy."

"No last name?"

"Not on this trip." She pretends to take another sip of her beer, which has been empty for who knows how long, so she can avoid his gaze. She wonders why she doesn't want to look at him, but the question lingers only a moment before she pinpoints the answer.

Because she likes him. He's charming, sweet, and honest. *Damn.* Liking him is one thing—letting him control your emotions and vacation is another.

Tingles rise from her stomach to her head. She excuses herself to the restroom so she can regroup.

She slithers off the stool, but her dress catches the edge as she slides down. In an instant, he reaches down to grab her arm. She mumbles, "thank you," and weaves her way in and out of the tables and chairs, avoiding the gaze of the other patrons in case they saw her nearly fall. She's sure his eyes burn into her ass as she walks away.

Chapter Seven
Change of Plans

The restroom smells like cheap baby powder air freshener. She breathes through her mouth so she doesn't gag. She goes into a stall and shakes her head at the plastic flowers sitting on the back of the toilet. *That's fucking dumb. There are fresh flowers everywhere that would look much prettier.* Amy jumps when she's finished, surprised by the loudness of the flush. Water from the toilet leaves small water spots on her dress. *Fuck. Now he's going to think I pissed myself.* Shaking her head, she stares at herself in the mirror, red lipstick in hand. *I want to fuck him. I'm going to fuck him. No. Yes. Why not? You deserve a good time.* Just don't get too involved. Get what you want, then be done.

He isn't Alejandro, and besides, he said he's divorced. It'll be an excellent distraction from that stupid book.

Alejandro. Only three months ago, but it feels like a lifetime.

****

Cabo San Lucas was with all her favorite girlfriends—her sister, Ava, Lexi, Natalie, and Emma. Katy was sorely missed because she'd died before they were able to take that trip together again. The partying got old, so Amy decided to go scuba diving—and give

42

her liver a break. For all her ex-husband's faults, he had encouraged her to get certified, and if for nothing else, she was grateful. It was her first trip as a single woman. Although the divorce papers were not yet signed, she'd already moved out and was mentally checked out, done with him, with no hope for a reunion. Ever. If she was lucky. But let's be honest, she'd been done even before meeting Kevin.

The soft hangover snores of her friends hung in the air as she grabbed her gear to go diving. She walked to the marina and mumbled to herself about how different this city was in the morning. At night, people walked from bar to bar, hooting and hollering the way drunk people do. But in the early morning, the quiet made Cabo seem less like a party town, and the smell of the saltwater was welcome compared to the usual alcohol, sweat, vomit, and overused sewer scents that normally assaulted her nose at night.

When she arrived at the dive center, she introduced herself to the dive master, Alejandro. He was a cute twenty-something man. His coppery skin, a thick accent, and muscular calves made him sexy as fuck.

While Amy hadn't planned on being the only diver, it appeared she was the only one. *This is unusual. I've never been diving where the dive master was also the boat captain.* Cheap bastards.

The way he pronounced her name gave her shudders. He elongated the *y* at the end, making it sound much prettier than in English. Alejandro inquired in his adorable accent, "Why are you here alone?"

"I am here in Cabo with my friends, but none of them are scuba divers." He nodded, and he helped her put on the rental gear. His hands lingered a bit too long on her hips, fitting her for a weight belt. When he turned her around to face him, his hand brushed her breast. Her nipples were called to attention. *It was a fucking accident.* Just chill out. *He's just trying to make sure everything fits.* Her gaze flashed at his bare ring finger.

He described the dive site they'd visit, called "Neptune's Finger," just outside of the marina. *Focus, Focus.* He explained he'd drive out there, jump in the water to connect to the buoy, and then they'd dive. At this dive site, there was a phenomenon called a "sand falls," which is a place where the ocean triples in depth and the sand falls into the abyss. *Like how I used to be.*

Amy boarded the boat after the briefing with her rented gear, and Alejandro followed. *I hope my thighs aren't too jiggly.* She almost wished she'd rented a wet suit to hide her tummy and thighs. *But wet suits are gross. Ugh, all the people who peed in them before me. No thank you.*

They pulled out of the marina, and her heart quickened at the sight of Arco del Cabo and Lover's Beach, even though it was the third time. The vastness of the ocean behind the rock formation arch and the pure white sand was the stuff of postcards.

This was the first time she'd been back after being in Cabo with her ex-husband, and Katy the time before that. *Sure wasn't a lovers' beach for me.* Why did they fight that day? She couldn't remember the specifics since it was such a common occurrence. *I'm sure it was something stupid I did that he didn't like.*

At the dive spot, Alejandro dove into the water. She watched him swim toward the buoy, his skin glistened in the sun. Without thinking, she jumped into the ocean, wanting to taste the salt on her lips. She popped out of the water and gasped, filling her lungs with air—the water was colder than she expected.

"Hey, Amy, you can't be out here yet." He looked away from the buoy, shouting to her.

She laid flat, eyes closed, and her face dried instantly from the tropical sun. The ocean waves lapped over her ears, so she pretended as if she didn't hear him.

Alejandro swam to her and winked. "You're naughty. You can't be out here yet." *Naughty.* That's a weird word to use. She tingled down to her toes.

She ignored him and continued to float. *He can't tell me what to do.* I'm a free woman now. I do what I want. He climbed the ladder and offered a hand that she didn't take. *If I want to swim, I'll swim.* Taking her sweet time, she finally joined him on the boat.

They both got their gear on, and she watched him out of the corner of her eye as he slid the wet suit over his middle and pulled it up over his arms. The tight garment outlined his package. She stared too long, and her chest flushed.

Once they were ready, they both jumped in, put the regulators in their mouths, and sank.

Hundreds of colorful fish surrounded her. She swam around the rock formation, following Alejandro, her muscles and body loosening in the zero gravity she loved.

Then there were loud sounds, like a dog barking. *What the fuck is that?* Amy's heart pounded because who wasn't a bit afraid of sharks? Then she saw the figures. Four of them darting in the water, almost as if they were dancing. She squints to make them out, and they were sea lions. *Oh my God! Holy shit. Sea lions. I must have built up good karma somewhere.* Amy and Alejandro watched them play for the whole dive, one of them even nibbling on her fins. *They're just like dogs.* A tinge of sadness set in. She missed her Casey.

Alejandro pointed to his air and gave a thumbs-up to show it was time for them to rise. Upon surfacing, she took in gulps of the fresh ocean air.

"That was amazing."

"It was. The sea lions seldom leave Lover's Beach and come this far. This is only the second time I've seen them out here."

Yeah, karma.

Alejandro swam to the buoy to unhook the boat while she floated faceup, deep in thought, saltwater droplets burning her lips.

When they were back in the boat, she asked Alejandro about the sea lions. Like the National Geographic channel, he told her what they eat and when they mate and how one of them, Poncho, sometimes boarded fishing boats that came into the marina in the evenings. *Someone else passionate about the ocean. So fucking hot.*

Amy moved across the bow to brush the tangles out of her hair. Big knots on her locks always happened when scuba diving. *Long hair is nice, but what a fucking pain sometimes.* She winced when she pulled too hard and got a brush full of her hair. Alejandro watched her, and she avoided eye contact with him in what seemed like a private moment.

Between the nitrogen gas and the sea lion encounter, she was giddy.

"We have some time. Would you like to go over to

Arco del Cabo?"

"Sure." Feigning that she couldn't see over the boat's windshield, she jumped up to join him on the captain's chair, which was just wide enough for two people. Single life had made her braver. She put her hand on his muscular inner thigh, covered by the wet suit. He looked at her and grinned.

Skimming the top of the water, the motor slowed as it reached the sand. She didn't wait for the boat to stop before she jumped off the stern of the boat.

He yelled, "Stop." It was futile. "You take too many risks." Alejandro cut the engine and got the ropes ready to tie the boat to shore.

Amy wasn't sure if he was joking or not as she bobbed on top of the water, waves getting saltwater into her mouth and nose. "You have no idea." A chuckle erupted from her because she was the most in-control person she knows—and never took risks and overthinks everything. Always. Always in control. She liked this new girl, though. Maybe she'd keep her around for a while.

Once he tied off the boat, they strolled on the beach, the waves crashing at their feet. The silence between them allowed her to focus on the seaweed smell entering her nostrils.

Unable to resist, she waded out into the water until she was waist-deep, and Alejandro followed. An unexpected wave came toward them, and she squealed and ran away from it, but he grabbed her by the waist from behind to keep her steady. "Running from the wave is bad. You'll get knocked over." She turned to thank him, and his breath was hot on her mouth.

He held her gaze. His intense black eyes seemed

darker in the scorching sun. He grabbed her neck and pulled her close. His breath smelled like saltwater as he pulled her in for a kiss. She kissed him, and the early morning rush of wild animals and the ocean created excited dizziness. His lips were salty, and the warmth of his mouth on hers sent heat down to her toes and pulsating in her pussy.

His powerful arms. His exploring lips. His look of desire. Her back arched. *I need him.* Playing hard to get, she pulled away from him and walked out toward the water, grabbing his hand to encourage him to come with her. He followed, clasping his hands around hers, strong. He nipped on her lips, teasing, and pushed his exploring tongue inside her fiery mouth.

Standing on her tiptoes, she reached for his crotch. His cock grew through his wet suit. *Let's be honest, you've been wanting to do this all morning.* The thought of taking that inside her filled her with delicious anticipation. She gave his cock a gentle squeeze through the wet suit.

He removed her hand, put her arms at her sides, and reached his hand down into her swimsuit bottom. Her pussy responded to his probing fingers, and her clit throbbed for him. She swelled, her pussy red hot for more. She was exhilarated. She squirmed, and he purred, "I'm going to make you come."

He pushed his fingers inside her and didn't release eye contact. She reached for his dick, but he moved her hand away, again.

"Today is for you." He worked his thumb on her clit while exploring two fingers deep into her pussy. She gasps deep breaths to fill her lungs and had difficulty remaining steady, his fingers pushed in her most private area. She relinquished control and pushed her hips into the rhythm of his fingers, grabbing his shoulders for leverage. She wished she could say that was the first time she'd had such an encounter with a stranger. It wasn't, and she never believed she needed to apologize for her sexuality. Well, at least until she had those encounters when she was married, with Kevin. Moaning under his breath, he pulled his fingers from inside her and gestured toward the boat.

She sighed. Frustrated. *I hope he isn't done yet.*

She took the first step on the boat ladder and was shaky from his fondling. He reached his hand out to steady her on the steps. This time, she accepted it.

She hadn't reached the top of the ladder, when his voice boomed as he looked at her, "You've been naughty today. Do you know what I do with naughty girls?"

"What?" Amy choked, breathless, on her word. She attempted not to slip into the water. *Oh God, please tell me.* Her belly clenched, excited and nervous.

"I will tie you up. Do you like that?" He released her hand, nudged her to sit on the captain's chair, grabbed a rope from a storage area under the seat, and tied her hands together in a perfect handcuff knot.

"Yes," she squeaked, giddy and yearning.

He held the rope tight around her wrists with one hand and used his other hand to yank at her swimsuit bottom, pulled it around her ankles. Then he pushed her thighs apart. Her cunt was fully exposed for his playing and probing. Normally, she might be embarrassed about this, it was daylight, after all. But today, she was a different woman. A brave one. A naughty one. One that deserved to have him pay tribute to her pussy.

He fondled the lips of her pussy, making small circles with his finger, and Amy squirmed, wanting him to put his fingers inside her. She lusted for him. For more. For release. He grabbed the rope harder, increasing the tension so his power was clear. She melted into the cheap faux leather seat. *Take me.*

Understanding, Alejandro released the tension and explored her pussy with both hands. He put his thumb on her clit while pushing two fingers into her saturated cunt. She mouthed to herself, *Find my spot.* She pushed her hips toward his fingers until he found it. She moaned.

"You like that?" It was more of a statement than a question. Her pussy was dripping wet.

"Yes." She squirmed. His finger-fucking became more and more rapid. The pressure on her clit combined with his probing fingers in her pussy made her back arch, and she became dizzy with waves of pleasure. The sensation of a stranger's fingers inside of her was intoxicating. It also made her forget about the pain of the last year. All she had to do was focus on her own pleasure with a stranger.

"Hold still." He grabbed the rope and tightened it. "A naughty girl needs to obey and come when I tell her to come."

Yes, I'll do what you say. Anything you say. Nervousness subsided, replaced with thrilling exuberance.

Then he put his mouth between her legs, holding the rope tight with one hand. Her tied hands hung rigid at her side. His tongue moved in small circles around her pussy lips, and he thrust three fingers into her and flicked her clit with his tongue. It was likely there were already red marks appearing on her back from the captain's chair. The thought of this was thrilling and created throbbing in her pussy, needy for more.

He moved his fingers in a twisting motion, in and out, and he pulled his mouth away to watch himself banging her cunt. It was sexy to see him panting as he watched. As her pussy got wetter, his thrusts matched the puffing of a faraway boat engine. Her heart seemed to beat out of her chest, and she leaned her head on the headrest, allowing waves of pleasure to take over, knowing she was close.

He took out his fingers and, in one move, penetrated her with his tongue, flicking in and out, around, and around. He tightened his hold on the rope. Her thighs stiffened. Her wetness had seeped onto the cushion. He mouth-fucked her quicker, finding the spot that made her whine and added a finger, banging that sweet spot while flicking her clit with his tongue.

She ruptured, the rush of orgasm matching the sound of the waves crashing against the boat. Her entire body ignited, and she shuddered. The rope tightened against her wrists, stinging. Redness appeared. Bad and painful memories disappeared. There was nothing else than the shuddering of her body and the freedom of release.

Alejandro came up for air and withdrew his fingers. She sighed, missing their presence, shutters still pulsating throughout her body.

He was the first to speak. "Did you like that?"

"Oh yes." He untied her wrists. She reached for his dick, which pushed against his wet suit, stiff. *I need to put my mouth on that cock.*

"No." He pulled away. "Today is for you. I hope

you learned a lesson about following the rules. Naughty girls that don't follow the rules get tied up. Next time you're naughty, I may have to put you over my knee, then fuck the naughty out of you."

She was breathless, visualizing that picture. Breaking the rules with him sounded thrilling.

He grabbed her swimsuit bottom and knelt in front of her and worked the sticky material back on her. Although her swimsuit was still wet, her pussy was wetter.

When they arrived at the marina, Alejandro told her how much he enjoyed diving with her with a glint in his eye because the office manager was watching.

"It was a great dive." She handed him a twenty-dollar tip.

"I can't accept this because it was my pleasure." He handed the money back to her.

She walked to the hotel and, without hesitation, scheduled a scuba dive for the next day. She planned to scuba diving every day for the rest of her trip, distracting herself from spending time with her friends, which had been the whole reason for going. Although they had all lost their friend Katy, Amy didn't want to talk about it with anyone. She and Alejandro had gone beyond just fucking. She shared private things with him, like her fears and past. She'd been open with him about Katy.

Amy talked with him and had the naughty fucked out of her rather than drinking it away or crying about it with her best friends for the entire week. Being with Alejandro and having him inside her was a welcome distraction. That was until she and her friends were shopping in town one morning. As they walked in and out of the cheesy tourist shops, she spotted Alejandro walking on the other side of the street. She raised her arm to wave at him until her stomach dropped. He held hands with a Mexican woman, her chiseled features more pronounced because of the crown of straight black hair that reached her breasts. Two kids were in tow.

The sun caught the diamond on her ring finger as they walked. A young boy about six yanked at Alejandro's shorts, and he bent down to talk with him, and they hugged. The girl, maybe three or four years old, held her mom's hand and shouted, in a bratty tone, "But Mommy, I really want to go." *He didn't tell me he was married. With kids. Fucker.* Although Amy knew they were just having casual sex, she still felt betrayed by his leaving this important bit of information out. She'd told him private things, and she thought he'd told her private things. She canceled her scuba dive for the next day and, for the rest of the trip, wallowed in disappointment. Her friends assumed she was sad because of Katy. She'd hoped he was different. Not that she expected to have a long-distance relationship with him or anything, but she expected honesty, especially after she'd been so open and vulnerable with him.

****

Distant voices coming closer bring her back to reality. When the voices enter the ladies' room, she realizes she is still standing in front of the mirror, lipstick in her hand. She has no idea how long she'd been daydreaming.

The women are loud and stumble their way in, smiling at her. She smiles, puts lipstick on, straightens her posture, and returns to the thatched-roofed bar. She finds Parker staring at her, and she smiles. Seeing him erases all memories of Alejandro and Cabo. She wants him.

His subtle smile and the way he eyes her with desire make the decision easy about hooking up with him. *Fuck what happened with Alejandro. It was a fluke.* Besides, even the best-laid plans change sometimes. And end better than expected. Just maintain control around him—don't tell him anything. Use it for what it is. Just sex. She wishes she could think of a recent example of something ending better than expected but can't. There goes that negativity again.

When she returns, Parker doesn't hide the ogling of her cleavage, and his gaze rests on hers. "I'm not even going to ask you what took so long. Do you want to walk on the beach?"

"With a stranger? I don't know how safe that is," she teases.

"Well, we've pretty much shared life stories, so I expect it's safe. But what fun would it be without a little danger?" His eyes gleam.

I'm just going to go for it. What's the worst that could happen? I get laid, then enjoy the rest of my vacation sexually satisfied? I'll take that chance. There is just one rule. Don't get attached.

Chapter Eight
The Beach Walk

She wants to pounce on him now that the decision is made but plays coy instead. She takes a large gulp of her beer, allowing his question to hang in the air for a few moments. "You're right. Let's do it."

He releases a large breath.

She grabs for the check, but Parker stops her and pays.

"I've got this."

Whatever. He doesn't know he's going to get laid. Let him pay for it. I hope he tips well.

The bartender winks at Parker. *Well, that's bullshit. What, is that guy code?*

Parker hands her another beer, explaining, "It's a roadie."

"I like the way you th—" She doesn't finish her sentence. Moonlight dancing on the ocean catches her attention.

Once they're down the stairs, the breeze catches her hair, and strands stick to her lipstick. *I hate that.* Parker reaches for her hand. She pulls her hand away and gathers her hair, groping for the hair band around her wrist. Balancing the beer between her legs, she puts her hair in a messy ponytail.

"What, you don't want to hold my hand?"

"This isn't a date." The corners of her lips tease

him.

"Isn't it? I invited you for drinks, we talked, and now we're walking on the beach. That's pretty much the definition of a date. A romantic one, if I do say so myself."

Fuck, he isn't wrong. Especially about the romantic part. "Well, I prefer to move slow."

"Do you? Somehow I doubt that." His eyes crinkle again.

Amy clenches her thighs. Even though she already decided to fuck him, she loves the flirty dance that comes with meeting someone new and knowing— before they do—they'll be inside of her. It's like those penguins that try and find the perfect rock to give to the penguin they want to be their mate or that other bird that dances around the potential partner in the hopes of impressing her. It's just a quick relationship built on sex. *He'll go home, I'll go home, and I will have had some fun. No harm in that.*

She grimaces as she loses her balance on a piece of driftwood. Parker grabs her elbow to steady her. His biceps brush her bare arms, and goose bumps appear on her skin. *He didn't notice.*

She takes off her flip-flops and carries them in the same hand as her beer, which is almost empty. She takes cigarettes out of her bag and leans down low, lighting it near her chest to avoid the wind.

"What, you smoke?" He raises his eyebrows.

"Obviously." She's annoyed. *This is my vacation. I can smoke if I want. I will never let another man tell me what to do.* Unsure of where this strong feeling came from, she gives him the benefit of the doubt. *He was just surprised since I didn't smoke in front of him at the bar.*

"You're pretty much the last person to look like a smoker."

"What does a smoker look like?"

"I don't know, just, um…" He stammers. "Just not like you. I didn't mean to make it sound like I was judging."

She starts to explain that she only smokes on vacation…and evenings, then stops. *I don't owe him an explanation.*

Smoke fills her lungs, and she exhales. The smoke dances on the breeze. *Maybe it's dangerous to be out here with someone I just met.* The beach is dark and deserted. Her heart flutters.

Alejandro, Alejandro, Alejandro runs through her mind to the tune of an old eighties song. She decides at that moment to enjoy Parker's company and avoid any emotions for him. *It'll be what it will be, just fun sex. There. It's settled.* Even though it was already settled in the bathroom.

The sand is still warm from the sun. The splash of the gentle waves sounds like the station she listens to at home to fall asleep. A large ship in the distance honks its horn, low and friendly. They don't speak. Parker follows her to the water's edge. She dips her toes in the water, throws her cigarette in her beer can, *because littering is rude*, then tosses her beer, bag, and flip-flops on the beach without turning around to face him. In one move, she takes off her dress and push-up bra, throwing them aside. She wants to cover up her nakedness, but she doesn't because of the liquid courage, and runs toward the water because the ocean is calling her. The water reaches her waist, and before she can shiver from the cold darkness, she dives into the black water.

When she comes up for air, he's standing on the beach watching her, his mouth gaping open. Like she is always this impulsive, she smiles at him. Then she turns on her back and floats. The moon is full and bright and lights the beach, so she has a full view of Parker. *Shit, this is fucking colder than I thought.* Her nipples stand at attention.

"What the fuck are you doing? And you were nervous about walking on the beach with me? Do you know what's in the water at night?" His gaze shifts from side to side and out to the horizon.

"Okay, Safety Sam, you're the one who said nothing's fun without a little danger." She looks out toward the horizon, hiding a wince because he didn't jump in after her. The saltwater laps at her skin, and she splashes her exposed breasts with water. Don't ask him to come in.

"Come in. The water's fine." *I'm a fucking idiot.*

Unspeaking, Parker looks down the beach and out to the horizon. His black, country music T-shirt slips over his arms, and the breeze catches it as it drops. He has a large tattoo of a bear head on his chest. *As if I wasn't already hot for him because of his arms.* Tattoos—which often go along with the bad boy persona, the exact opposite of her ex-husband—have always been attractive to her. *If I knew that, why did I marry him to begin with?* She pushes that thought away so she can concentrate on him. She makes a mental note to ask him about the tattoo.

He unzips the fly on his pants before unbuttoning the top button. *Why do men always do that?* She licks her lips as he pulls down his jeans, moving one side down, then the other. When he reaches his thighs, his shaft pops out as he pulls them the rest of the way down. His dick stands at attention, the throbbing visible in the moonlight. His cock is thick, long, and calling for her to sit on it, lick it, suck it. Amy shudders. She can't remove her gaze from the way he moves. His stride is breezy, confident, shoulders are straight, as if he isn't naked in front of her. Self-assuredness is sexy. Not to mention the sexiness of his dick bobbing, calling to her, as he moves toward the water.

Parker first dips his toes in the water and gives her a pained look. He inhales a deep breath as if he is going under water and walks toward her, maintaining eye contact.

"This water isn't fine at all. It's cold," he whines.

"Oh, shut up and get out here." Amy rolls her eyes at herself. *Stupid response.*

He walks toward her, tentative, arms spread wide to keep balance. She yearns to stroke and claw his arms, his chest, and his thick cock.

She can feel the heat radiating from his body as he gets closer. He wraps his arms around her, and she wraps her legs around his torso, the bottom half of her body weightless in the water. His cock is like a lion unleashed, poking her inner thigh. Her pussy aches. Their mouths are inches apart, and he looks as if he is going to kiss her. His breath smells like the beer they'd just finished.

He takes an arm from around her shoulder and rubs his fingers against her nipple, then makes large circles around her breast. He leans in for the kiss she's been craving. The taste of the saltwater on his lips is refreshing when it lingers on her mouth. Shivers move down her spine.

His tongue explores her mouth, tentative at first, then growing needier. As he kisses her, she reaches down to touch his cock, which is now resting on the front of her thighs.

He moves her hand away and glances past her shoulder to the horizon. "Chilly water and shrinkage and all. My dick doesn't want you to have the wrong first impression."

Amy chuckles. His sense of humor and confidence is what makes her throb this time.

"You and your body make my cock hard, despite the shrinkage," he whispers in her ear, leaving her lips for a moment.

My body?

He takes both hands and grabs her tits, cupping them in his hands. She removes her legs from around his waist, missing his cock on her thigh.

"I want to feel you from the inside." He moves his fingertips from her breast and brushes her skin on the way down to her stomach. His fingers settle just above her clit. He puts his other hand behind her neck and tickles the hair on her nape. Mute, but inside, she screams for him to rub her clit with his other finger.

Tipsy and high on the saltwater and earlier sun of the day, her voice cracks. "Finger-fuck me."

He listens and pushes his thumb on her clit and bends down to move his other fingers inside her. He starts with one finger, then two, then three. Each additional finger brings a new uptake of breath.

"I want my cock in there," he whispers in her ear, then kisses her again. "But not just yet."

He explores her cunt, and she trembles. His pattern

and pressure are perfect, with his thumb rubbing her clit and his fingers in, out, in, out in solid movements. The saltwater sloshes around them, and the waves lapping at the sand are gentle and soft. The exact opposite of what she wants him to do to her. Her breathing comes faster. The water gets hotter, and she is dizzy, desire radiating from her toes to her head.

He stops, puts his arms around her, and kisses her again. This time, it's not the kiss of a man needing to plow her but the gentle kiss of a friend, except on the lips. She's frustrated. She needs more. Now.

She sees desire in his gaze and wonders why he stopped.

"My dick will be inside you when you come," he responds, a little too confident.

Exasperated, she exhales.

"Want to keep walking?"

Um, no, I want you to finish what you fucking started. "Sure." She eyes her dress in a pile on the sand.

They hold hands, their feet splashing as they make their way to shore. Amy shivers, unsure if it's from the promise of his dick inside her later or because it's breezy. He stares as she puts her push-up bra into position. The beer has made her less self-conscious about her body, and she bends over, staying there a second too long, then she picks up her dress, giving him a full view of her behind. She hears him whistle. She's satisfied. He shoves his dick back inside when he pulls up his jeans and buttons the top button before he zips.

"So you like country music?" she fills the silence, referring to the T-shirt. What a dumb comment. *How can I speak in front of a class of one hundred but can't think of anything clever to say one on one?*

"I do. I'm originally from the backwoods of Tennessee. What else am I supposed to like?" He chuckles. She picks up her flip-flops and walks ahead of him, still pulsating between her thighs. She strolls with flat, tentative feet to accommodate the wetness between her legs.

They walk for twenty minutes, turn around, head to the hotel, and are back to the small talk she hates. Favorite movie? Favorite band? Favorite food? *Stupid conversation*, but she isn't quite sure how to get to the deeper discussion like they had at the bar. That kind of chit-chat makes her excited, mentally...and physically. He doesn't grab her hand this time. She's disappointed.

Her face flushes, remembering how she fell on the stairs earlier as they approach the steps leading to the hotel. *Damn anxiety. But so far, I haven't needed the pills on this trip.* She glides up the steps, maintaining control, the beer swirling in her head.

The automatic sprinklers turn on under the palm trees, so she stares at the water instead of having to look at him. "Do you want to go to your room?"

"You're ready to be fucked with more than my fingers, then?"

Amy shifts her stance to look at him. His eyes crinkle, yet they're serious.

"Yes? Tell me how bad you want it." She can tell he's serious.

"I want you inside of me, bad." She licks her lips and doesn't move her gaze from his. Feigning confidence.

"I think you can do better than that. But that will do for now. Come to my room. Let's get a couple of beers on the way." He struts toward the bar.

The same bartender is working. Parker orders the beers, and as the bartender opens them, he glances at her damp hair.

"Go for a swim?" Jaden winks at Parker, and Parker winks back.

"We did, Jaden."

Of course they know each other. Parker has been working here for weeks.

Parker grabs the beers, hands her one, then puts his arm around her waist, reaching down to squeeze her ass.

"Have fun," Jaden calls to them as they walk toward Parker's room.

Parker reaches for her hand, and she takes it this time. Her beer is empty by the time they get to his room. Inside, everything is in order and immaculate. She resists the temptation to peek in the bathroom to see if he has his toiletries lined on a washcloth too. Warmth spreads in her chest. His room is decorated like hers, only smaller. Two overstuffed chairs are squished on the balcony, a fan whirs above the bed, and the same silky palm tree throw pillows on the bed.

"You're quite the housekeeper." It's the first thing that comes to her mind.

"Yeah, there are just a few things I like dirty."

She trembles. This time it's not because she's cold.

He fiddles with his phone, and country music comes on. Taking a step toward her, he unbuttons his jeans. The moonlight shines through the balcony slider, lighting his face.

"I want to see you undressed." He brushes against her, showing her to sit on the bed.

She sucks in her tummy and raises the dress over

her head, obeying his request. She shakes in anticipation when she unhooks her bra, and it falls on the bed next to her. Her gaze doesn't leave his. She glances at his cock, and she sees it stiff through his jeans. Standing there naked, she's exposed. Again. And doesn't care.

He reaches for her, sits on the bed, and runs his fingers down the shape of her hourglass body on both sides. His fingers are like Fourth of July sparklers on her skin. Amy moves closer to him, stands in front of him, and reaches for his shirt. She pulls it from the collar, careful not to turn it inside out as she looks at the bear tattoo again. She starts to ask him about it, but her craving for him is greater than her curiosity. *I'll ask later.*

She gets on her knees in front of him, her gaze locked on his. She unzips his taut pants, his hard cock poking against them. When she creeps his pants down his hips, he raises them so she can pull them to his knees. She inhales when his cock releases from his pants. It's even nicer up close.

Amy grabs his shirt and puts it between her knees and the blue tile floor for comfort. She raises her gaze toward him, and his eyes are closed, and his chest heaves. She takes his dick in her hand and rubs it from the shaft to the tip, then down. He moans and lies on the bed, his toes curling on the tile floor. She spits as quiet as she can for lubrication and gets a solid tempo going as she moves her hand on his cock, like a pro. His dick fills her palm. Her racing heart feels as if it will beat out of her chest, anticipating him inside her.

Without missing a beat, Amy opens her mouth wide to suck on the tip while groping his balls. There's pre-cum on the tip, and she licks it, hoping to get more of his sweet taste. He sighs and sits to face her.

"Put it all in your mouth." His voice cracks and he paws at her tits. She takes his dick inside her mouth and lets out an inaudible gag when his cock reaches the back of her throat. She sucks it while keeping her hand constantly twisting around his shaft. *Now, this I know I'm good at, even if I am out of practice.* It's like riding a bike.

The heat from his body makes her sweat, and the quick motion of her mouth moving up and down on his cock makes her boobs bounce together. He whimpers. She loves giving him pleasure and picks up the pace.

In one rapid motion, he grabs her under the arms and pulls her up. He stands next to her and pushes her legs apart, reaching down to slide a finger into her juice-soaked pussy.

"You're so wet." He's pleased.

Out of breath, Amy responds, "Yes."

"I want to fuck you. Can I fuck you hard?"

"Yes, I want that." She shivers from the eagerness of being filled by him.

He pushes her on the bed, his eyes questioning if this is okay. She moans to show him she likes him to take charge, which was a recent new experience with Alejandro. Her ex-husband would have never considered being dominant in bed, even though he was dominant everywhere else in their life. *I'm learning.* Relinquishing control, for once, puts her at ease. She lies down, her thighs spread so he can see her waxed pussy, and her gaze invites him inside her.

"No. Turn around."

Delighted, Amy flips around so she's on all fours,

her entire pussy open to him. She hopes her ample ass calls to him.

The crackle of a wrapper followed by the snap of a condom makes her jump.

He grabs her by the hips and gives her ass a small slap that sends shivers down her spine, anticipating what will come next. He shoves himself into her, all in one swift motion.

Amy gasps. Her cunt is like an inferno, filled with him.

His thick, pulsing cock penetrated her walls, pushing deep inside. Her pussy drips as he shoves himself in and out, in and out. A good, hard fucking is just what she was craving. It was a welcome distraction from the stupid book she was reading earlier. A reminder she was desirable despite what her ex-husband had told her. *Why am I thinking about my ex-husband?* She turns her attention to the scrumptious feel of him filling her, relentless and hard.

"Fuck yeah." He pounds her from behind. "You like this, don't you?" He's not expecting an answer. But her response, of course, would be yes.

She reaches to touch her swollen clit, sending tremors of pleasure down her body. He removes her hand. "Only I may pleasure you in the Bahamas tonight."

Oooh. I like the way this is going.

He grabs a fistful of her damp ponytail and pulls as his cock pounds inside her body. Bliss.

Her pussy is drenched and she needs to come. It's like a riptide pulling her under, making her out of control.

She touches her clit again, and in one rapid move,

he pulls his dick out, sits on the bed, and pulls her onto his lap, facedown. Her legs dangle, and her wetness drips down her thighs. In shock, she lets out a deep sigh in response.

"I told you, no touching yourself." She can hear his smirk. His cock is against her rib cage, and her only thought is wanting more of it.

"I will be easy with you this time, but next time, I won't."

She shudders in pleasure at what she hopes is about to happen. She's read about it, and the thought of it sends chills up her spine.

He raises a hand and smacks her hard on the ass. Quivers of pleasure radiate from her ass, which is, no doubt, rosy now. The sharp slap sets every nerve, especially those in her cunt, on fire. He slaps her other ass cheek, harder this time, and her pussy clenches uncontrollably.

"Promise me you will listen to me." He clears his hoarse voice.

"Yes, I promise I will listen to you."

"Do you know what happens if you don't?" It really isn't a question.

"What?" Amy closes her eyes, excited for his response.

"I'm going to paddle your ass, then I will fuck you in the ass."

She's never done that before, but the potential for that punishment causes her heart to flutter, and goose bumps appear on her arms.

Parker pulls her to her feet and lays her on her back. He spreads her legs apart and looks at her cunt. His cock pulsates, and he reaches toward his phone, which is still playing music. He turns up the volume, and a song about drinking beer on a Friday night screams from the phone's speaker like thunder, covering Amy's panting. The twang and words are familiar.

He comes to the bed and moves toward her on his knees, his dick bobbing. The condom is still on it.

"Can I take this off?" He raises his eyebrows.

Thinking of the birth control pill she takes every morning, and the conversation they'd had earlier about both of them being disease free, she answers almost before he's finished asking. "Yes." She wants to feel his bare skin inside of her. Besides, she trusts him.

He nods. He rips it off and throws it on the floor. He moves her legs as far apart as they will go and shoves himself into her, making her realize how much she missed the few minutes his cock was absent from her pussy.

He grabs her ponytail and thrusts into her. Then he removes his hand from her hair and vigorously rubs her clit until she's going to explode. Desperate for release, she meows like a kitten in the rain, "Can I come?" Her voice is soft and sheepish. She doesn't want to get in trouble again. Or maybe she does?

"I'm coming first, then you can. I'll tell you when."

He pulls both of her legs, so she's on her side, one leg on top of the other, exposing her pussy to him. He grabs a handful of her tits while holding her shoulder for leverage, pounding her.

"Here it is." He pounds into her harder. When he comes, it feels like a dam that has given way, hot cum shooting deep into her body. "Oh fuck." Shivers take over his body. He groans like an animal.

She's eager for her turn, and her voice wavers. "Can I come now?"

"Yes, you may." He pulls her legs flat on the bed and pushes her thighs apart. He inserts his cock in one deep push and brushes his lips on hers. He takes her hand and puts it on her clit, indicating she can pleasure herself while he fucks her. She rubs her clit, heat spreading throughout her body like wildfire.

The sensation of his cock penetrating the exact right spot as he pounds her harder brings her to the brink. She lets out a silent scream and is unconscious for several moments as the nerves throughout her body shiver, and she comes.

Amy closes her eyes to make the dizziness go away, unsure if it's from him or the alcohol. The world falls away. Parker lies down beside her and turns on his side to face her.

"How was that?"

"Mind-blowing." She turns her head to look at him.

"You're so sexy."

Of course, he's going to say that after we've just fucked. Amy answers with a mumble, "Thank you."

"Were you okay with the bossy stuff?" He smirks at her, already knowing the answer.

"I loved it. I've never really had someone boss me around like that." Even as she says it, she corrects herself in her head, since Alejandro was kind of like that.

"Me too. I also like it in reverse."

"Reverse?" she questions.

"You know, where you dominate me." He chuckles and looks at his toes.

"Oh yeah? I might be able to handle that." Prickles unexpectedly occur down below. *Maybe I can do that?* Her nerves tingle at the thought of sex beyond the traditional three positions she'd become used to while married. Even those three positions didn't happen very often, especially at the end.

He traces the curves of her breasts and hips without talking. Her breath slows to a normal pace.

"Do you want to stay here?" He gestures to the bed.

It's been a long time since she has slept in the same bed with anyone.

"I need to wash my face and brush my teeth, so I'm going to just head back to my room." She hopes he doesn't ask questions. She takes the question as a hint that he needs to go to sleep, so she gets up to put on her bra and dress. He watches her, his gaze not leaving hers.

"So what are you doing tomorrow?"

"I don't know yet." Amy skirts the question, remembering the promise to herself to not make this a "thing" ending with her being disappointed in him or their relationship, no matter how short lived it is to be. "Can I have your number?"

"I didn't get international phone service for while I'm down here," she lies.

"Okay, I'll just find you tomorrow when I'm off work."

She doesn't answer. *No commitment. This is just supposed to be easy, unemotional, and fun.*

Like a gentleman, he walks her to her room.

She's numb, in a good way. The deep sleep allows her to forget about the divorce, her cruel ex-husband, losing Katy, and the guilt of seeing Alejandro with his wife and kids. Sleep is mostly dreamless, except for Parker's face.

Chapter Nine
Rum and Punch

The next morning, her head pounds like it has its own heartbeat. Her eyes crusty, she tries to see the time but can't quite make it out. *I need coffee.* It is fortunate the nightstand is there as she needs to grab it to steady herself from the dizziness. The soreness between her legs causes a grin to spread across her face. She hasn't had hot sex like that since Kevin and Alejandro.

Sex with her husband was bland and mindless, until it disappeared altogether. Combined with the mean comments he'd always make, she reasoned she had a full life with her friends and work that she loved, and sex wasn't that important. Turned out that wasn't enough. Eventually the loneliness and lack of love gave way to seeking other options. Kevin, Alejandro, and now, Parker.

She turns her thoughts to her immediate need, coffee, and dials room service.

Drawn to the balcony, she grabs her laptop while she waits for room service. *Fucking email.* Clicking on Outlook, she sees the numerous messages from students and colleagues. After a quick glance through them, she decides fuck it. Yearning sets in. Yearning for a time when there wasn't so much technology to distract people from living life. She remembers as a little girl and visiting her dad at his office; there was no computer on his desk. Just stacks of paper. He never worked on weekends or during vacation. *How do we get back to that as a society?*

Taking a momentary stand against work-related technology, she googles "top country music" and listens to a few songs. *I still don't like it very much.*

Then she googles "how to be a sexually dominant female," and definitions of *dominatrix* appear and articles telling a female how to be dominant in the entire relationship with a husband or boyfriend. Then she finds an article that gives "50 Tips to Being More Dominant in the Bedroom," lights a cigarette, and begins reading. She rubs her eyes. The glare from the sun makes it hard to see, probably not helped by the amount of alcohol she consumed last night.

She is relieved when room service knocks. She pours a cup with a generous dose of cream, then settles down on the balcony. People drift to the pool, putting towels on their chairs to claim spots. *Annoying and rude.* Even though they're far below, their chatter and laughter drift upward. It's comforting.

She moves her laptop so there's less glare and continues reading the article. It talks about things like tying a man up to simple tactics like telling him what you want, such as, "No," "Put it there," "Slower," and "Faster." She shifts in her chair at the thought, ready for another round—or many more, with Parker.

After a minute, she realizes she's been staring into space. The whisper of palm fronds swaying in the wind fill her ears. Parker's name is on her lips, but she reminds herself the trip isn't all about him.

Rather than think about him all day, she goes to the concierge to see what kinds of tours they have. She doesn't shower to keep the aroma of Parker and sex on her body lingering in her nose all day.

She books a city and rum tasting tour.

"Don't you want to know the price?" The concierge questioned when she slid her credit card to him.

"It's okay. I know it's something I want to do." The day she realized she didn't have to worry about money so much was when she brought her paycheck stub home two years ago. Having been just promoted to associate professor, she'd earned a fat raise. When she'd handed the stub to her ex-husband, a smile creeped on her face. He sneered, tossed it back without a word about her raise, and demanded to know. "What's for dinner?"

Her eyebrows furrow over the control her ex-husband had over their money…and over her. She shakes his ever-present grimace from her memory.

"The tour leaves in an hour." The concierge slides her card over the mahogany desk.

Perfect, I have time for breakfast. "Thank you."

She smiles at the hostess when she enters the buffet restaurant. Her stomach flip-flops upon the competing scents assaulting her. Wanting to turn around and leave because of the hangover nausea, she decides she better eat.

A book comes to mind. A children's book, but not meant for children, about how the dad tries to get the kid to just fucking eat. She giggles while shoving down dry heaves as the hostess seats her. She and her friends read this book together every girl's weekend and fell into heaps of giggles. Usually after a few glasses of wine.

For a split second, she wishes one or all of her friends were here, experiencing this with her. *You're fucking trying to heal and need this fucking time alone.* Parker's face flashes. *Well, somewhat alone.*

Seated, the scent of bacon, which normally sends her swooning, ties her stomach in knots. Instead of eating, she takes her book out of the bag to read. *Damn it.* It's the one about the two best friends that made her sad before. *I meant to grab the other one.* After reading a chapter, a server passes, waffles and eggs waft toward her and doesn't make her want to retch. She plods to the buffet, grabbing a little bit of everything.

Slight bites go down easier while she's engrossed in her book.

In chapter six, one of the best friends gets married, and the other friend is happy for her. Unlike her best friend, right before Amy's wedding, Katy had looked at her, eyes sad. "Sure you want to do this?" Katy knew the man she was about to marry would likely become an ex-husband; it was just a matter of time. At the end of her marriage and the end of Katy's life, Amy tried to tell her she was leaving him. Her body was so full of a cocktail of medications, she wasn't sure Katy understood. Slamming the book shut erases the thought.

The chatter in the restaurant is light, and the laugher is booming. Irritated at happy people, she stifles tears. When her half-eaten plate of food is taken away, she smiles and drops her gaze to the floor, and leaves a ten-dollar tip out of guilt.

The short bus picks her up out front. The welcoming smiles of the tour guide and bus driver and the almost deafening chatter on the bus help her to forget about the stupid book. Weaving past the people already in their seats, she focuses on two women sitting near the back. They're giggling and whispering to each other as they look out the window. Amy turns to see what they're giggling about, and there's a cute valet at the curb, smiling at the women.

Both women are pretty and younger than her.

"You think everyone is pretty." Katy always told her.

"I know, I just believe in straightening each other's crowns and all that bullshit." They'd shared a smile. Katy knew her better than anyone.

Amy moves down the aisle and sits behind them. They both smile at her as she passes, stopping their roadside flirting with the valet for a second.

The tour guide explains they'll drive through downtown, and she'll point out the major sites. Then they'll do rum tasting at Graycliff, where they specialize in pairing chocolate and rum. *Fucking yum.* She is thankful she forced herself to eat, as the food cured her spinning head.

One of the women in front of her speaks so fast it takes a second for Amy to process what she said. "Does it get better than rum *and* chocolate?" Both women boom laughter, as if they'd already had a few drinks. Amy chuckles with them, and they turn, peering at her in the space between the ripped and dirty faux leather seats. She averts her eyes, embarrassed.

"Right?" She smiles, cheeks warm.

"Right? Screw the city tour. Let's get right to the rum." The dark-haired woman's grin is devilish.

"Right?" *You just said that, dumbass.*

"Where are you from?" the red-haired woman inquires.

"Washington State. What about you?"

"I'm from Oshkosh, Wisconsin." The dark-haired woman points to herself. "And she was from there until she got an awesome new job and moved away from me to Chicago."

"I love Chicago." A flood of memories washes over her. She and Katy had spent a weekend there for a conference where Amy was presenting research. Amy skipped most of the sessions so she and Katy could explore the city together. They shopped, compared pizza restaurants, and even rocked out at a Goo Goo Dolls concert at the Huntington Bank Pavilion. *Well, rocked out as much as you can to Goo Goo Dolls.* That was before they knew Katy was sick. Katy wanted to go home with a tan, so she hadn't worn sunscreen while sitting by the pool.

Anger wells. *Stupid. Katy. That was so fucking stupid.*

When the skin cancer metastasized to other parts of her body, including her brain, Katy was confident in her life choices.

"I don't regret anything. I'd still tan with no sunscreen and go to tanning beds. Because I looked *gooooood.* But I want you to promise me you'll wear sunscreen from now on."

Fucking bitch. So selfish. Angry tears well. *There's no crying on vacation,* Amy tells herself, unable to remember what movie that was from.

"I'm Jennifer." The red-haired woman tries to push her hand between the seats to shake it, but it gets stuck for a second. Their gaze meets and they both chuckle.

Amy introduces herself.

The dark-haired woman just smiles. "I'm Lynn."

The tour guide waves at them, her eyebrows furred in irritation, so the two women turn around, face the front, and the tour guide relates the history of Nassau and the Bahamas. Amy looks out the window at the people running errands, racing down the streets on bicycles, and her thoughts turn to Parker. *There's just something about him.* Maybe it's his self-confidence without being cocky.

She presses her lips together, blank gaze, not seeing the passing scenery through the window. *I like the way I am around him. I'm brave and impulsive. I wonder what he's doing tonight.* She blinks long, forcing those thoughts from her head. *This will not be a fucking thing.*

Still deep in thought, she is surprised when the tour guide announces, "We're here."

She gets off the bus last and lingers at the gates, taking in the salmon and white-colored British Colonial-style building, which is now a hotel and restaurant. She snaps a couple of pictures, sends a group text to her girlfriends, and adds, "I found my new house." She puts a smiley face at the end, as she does with most non-work-related texts. Jennifer and Lynn also linger, pointing out the gardens that line the pathway to the grand entrance.

They gawk at the colorful tropical flowers, and Lynn says, "Can you believe they have flowers growing here in December?"

"It's incredible." Amy ogles at them. "What I wouldn't give for some color at home this time of year. Everything is so gray in my neck of the woods."

"Yeah, ours too." Lynn walks faster to catch up with the group that's gathered just inside the lobby.

The tour guide recounts the history of Graycliff, explaining a famous pirate built the mansion, and goes on to talk about the long history of pirates in Nassau. She stares at the guide, making just enough eye contact so the guide thinks she's listening. But she's occupied with thoughts of last night. Still.

The guide leads the group to the chocolate tasting room, where samples are ready for them. Heavy wood chairs are reminiscent of years past, and the silky red and yellow tablecloths make the place seem elegant. The dozen or so chocolates are lined up on saucers, and the glasses of rum each have just a splash in them. People scatter trying to figure out where to sit. She eyes a table in the corner for two and beelines toward it. Jennifer grabs Amy by the arm and pulls her toward the women. "Sit with us."

She lets out an audible sigh. It'll be nice to not have to sit alone. "Thank you." She beams at Jennifer.

The manager explains the chocolate and the process of making it, then how pairing it enhances the flavor of the rum. He invites them to try the rum and chocolate bites. The three women clink their glasses and take their samples like shots and make small talk about their jobs and kids.

Lynn inquires, "Are you here alone?"

"I am. My divorce was finalized in November, and I needed a vacation."

"That's ballsy. I don't think I could travel alone." Lynn twists her hands together on top of the table.

"I don't know if it's ballsy as much as I just wanted to get away, and none of my friends were able to come. It's strange to eat alone and have drinks by the bar alone, though. Thanks for inviting me to sit with you.

It's nice to have some company."

"Well, I could see where it'd be lonely, but I think it's brave." Jennifer signals the manager and questions the other two women which rum was their favorite and orders another round.

Brave. Hmmm. Interesting word. *I'm calculating and thoughtful.* Not brave. This time, rather than in tiny glasses, the rum comes in whiskey-type glasses. When the manager sets them down, the crystal glasses form rainbows that dance on the windows. All three women clink their drinks together and shoot the rum again.

The manager raises his nose. "Why are you shooting them? You need to sip them, like a fine wine." She and the other two women giggle and order another round. Then, the tour guide announces they have an hour to explore the grounds.

"Want to just stay here?" Jennifer shoots them a devilish grin.

"Hell yes." They order another shot, chatting for the next hour. The volume of their conversation rises with every sip of rum they take.

"So have you met anyone interesting here? A single, pretty woman like yourself… I'd be surprised if you hadn't." Jennifer gives Amy a sideways glance.

"In fact, I have." She tells the women about Parker. Pretending she's always brave and impulsive, she talks about jumping in the ocean naked and how they ended up in his room.

"Oooooh fun. Are you going to see him later?"

"I don't know. I was hoping for an uncomplicated vacation, you know? I just don't know if I need the distraction."

"Fuck that. It's a vacation, and it doesn't have to be

complicated. Just fuck him and have fun. Go home and never think about him again. You just went through a divorce?"

"Yeah, I did."

"So you haven't had sex in a long time, right?"

"Well, not exactly." She laughs.

"You slutty bitch," Jennifer jokes. Under most circumstances, this coming from a stranger would make her uncomfortable, but it reminds her of the way she and Katy often teased each other. She warms, and her heart smiles.

"No matter what, I think you should fuck the shit out of him," Lynn chimes in.

"I probably will." Amy casts her gaze downward.

Jennifer tells Amy she got divorced about a year ago and the battle she's had with her ex over custody of their two small kids. Lynn tells her about her marriage, which appears to be hanging by just a string. She loves this kind of connection; these women are already like old friends. She loves the way Jennifer and Lynn finish each other's sentences and look at each other before they say something. Amy feels nostalgic.

Lynn pulls her phone out. "Oh shit. It's been over an hour. We gotta go."

"Damn." She slams back the rest of her rum. They pay and hurry to catch the short bus.

The glares of the other tourists on the bus are easy to ignore because of the rum. Under any other circumstance, she'd be horrified at being late and inconveniencing others. Lynn and Jennifer's giggles make her laugh too, which makes the other tourists frown even more.

The three of them hug when they reach Amy's

hotel. They exchange numbers, promising to meet later in the week.

****

When she arrives in her room, she opens the fridge. The cool air that blows on her face is welcome after the stuffy, sweltering bus ride. She grins to see the fridge has been restocked. She makes a mental note to leave a tip for the housekeepers in the morning. New beers every day, fresh towels, and a made bed? *I could fucking get used to this.* She grabs a beer and her pack of cigarettes and makes her way to the balcony. The sun is setting, and the orange-and-red sky makes the ocean flicker red-blue like a million diamonds.

Because her sister is a worrywart, she pulls her phone out to let Ava know she's doing fine. While her sister is too anxious about things, she needn't be concerned about her like she used to. It had taken two bottles of wine after an evening at Ava's for her to fully understand this. Her sister told her she thought Amy's ex-husband was mentally abusive and reminded her of several instances where Ava was a witness. Amy needed to know. "Why did you wait to tell me this until I'd left him?"

Ava looked at her. Her mouth was turned down at the corners and her eyes glistened. "Would you have listened?"

No.

Amy had turned away from Ava to hide her tears. His common ways of speaking with her came rushing like the powerful water on Niagara Falls. Like an old 1940s movie, the floodgate of insults comes back to her.

"You're so stupid."

"If only you were skinnier, I'd want to have sex with you more often."

"That's not how it happened; your memory is bad."

"Why aren't you ever nice to me?"

"Well, if you weren't so needy."

"Your success is a result of me supporting you. There's no way you could've done it on your own."

"Oh, my sweet chubby bear, you tried. But it just wasn't good enough."

"Why can't you do anything right?"

"Don't embarrass me."

Then there was the eye-rolling. Loud sighing. And constant smirking whenever she'd tell him something important to her. It wasn't until the conversation with her sister she realized that maybe, just maybe, this wasn't normal. She'd been living in a private hell she'd mistaken as heaven. She had heaved and sobbed in Ava's arms for what seemed like hours.

She had pulled herself together, vowing to never, ever make that mistake again. And accept that kind of treatment as normal.

Ava had petted her hair with long, gentle strokes until Amy calmed down. Finally, Ava answered in a low voice. "It was the quiet acceptance you had for the situation that was the most concerning." She continued to stroke her hair. "That August day you told me you'd left him was literally one of the happiest days of my life."

She shakes her head from gut-wrenching thoughts of her ex and texts her sister.

—*Hey, sis, wanted to let you know all is well.*— She sends a picture of the sunset to Ava.

—*Are you getting lots of pool time and sun?*—

83

—*Oh yes, and more.*— Amy adds a smiling devil face at the end of the text.

—*Oh yeah? Go sis. Just be careful.*—

She sends another smiley face in response. Ava is the best.

After smoking a few cigarettes, she walks to the closet to change for a walk around the resort, but there's nothing she feels like wearing. *I'm not looking for Parker or anything.*

She chuckles at how she is at bullshitting herself. Unsure of her plan, she scans her clothing options and chooses an off-the-shoulder top and a pair of denim shorts that hug her ass. One last check in the mirror, she stares into her own eyes for longer than necessary, checking her makeup and hair. An awkward moment. She sees a combination of her real self and the unattractive woman and unlikeable person she had been told she is. Yet somewhere deep, there's no way that can be true.

Down in the lobby, Amy looks around and sees Parker straight away. He's leaned back in his chair, moving his hands like he's telling a story to the colleagues next to him. They all stare at him intently.

She flushes, hoping the story isn't about her. Parker stops waving his arms when he spots her, and all the men turn to look at where he's staring. He stares at her, lingering at her breasts, and rests his gaze on her face. The butterflies rise in her belly.

"Good evening," she says, walking up to the group. She makes eye contact with each of the men, then holds Parker's gaze, and her eyes flash wide at the memory of the swat on the ass he gave her last night. Heat swells in her clit.

"How was elevator work today?" She takes her room key out of her back pocket.

"Good," one of the men answers, "we're almost done and get to go home soon."

Parker grins and rests his gaze on her breasts, the bra doing its job by creating a massive amount of cleavage. "What are you doing later?"

She leans over to whisper to him, pressing her room key in his hand. "You. Room 1186."

"I'll be there," he whispers in her ear, his breath hot.

"Have a good night." She meets their gaze and is careful to hold her head high when she strides away.

Shit. Now, I don't have a key. That was fucking stupid. She goes to the front desk to have them make her another one, less embarrassed at her mistake than she would've been a few months ago.

Amy shuffles to her room with the new key. She thinks of what Lynn had told her. "I think you should fuck the shit out of him." She smirked at her forwardness.

I fucking plan on it.

She decides what to wear when he arrives in her room. The problem is, she doesn't know if it will be in ten minutes or two hours. She gets naked and puts on a robe. Then she takes off the robe, *that looks fucking stupid*, and puts her shorts and top back on. The shorts are tight around her waist, *damn you, sweet rolls*, so she takes those off and slips on her swimsuit cover-up. It drapes around her middle but has a deep *V* showing her cleavage. *This is about as good as it gets.*

She fiddles with her laptop, reading more about dominance from the article she found earlier. *What if he catches me reading this*? She slams the laptop closed and lights a cigarette instead and paces the length of the balcony. Leaving her cigarette on the balcony, she grabs a beer from the fridge. She swallows quickly, then catches herself.

I don't want to be tipsy when he gets here. Her stomach does flips, so she just pounds the beer and goes inside for another. Then there's a click at the door, followed by a beep. Her stomach tightens. *Why did the door beep? Shit, they made me a new key, so the code is different. Fuck, why didn't I think of that?*

She rushes to open the door. He smiles when he sees her.

"The key didn't work."

"Sorry, I had to get a new key."

He doesn't respond and walks into the room.

"Fuck, this is a nice suite." He takes in the room and thrusts a drink in her hand. The pink umbrella in the drink stands at attention, and the tropical fruit floating in it reminds her of "jungle juice," the punch she used to make for high school parties in the woods in Spokane. *Yum.* His gaze questions whether or not she likes this. "I know we were mostly drinking beer last night, but a pretty woman needs a pretty drink occasionally. It's rum punch."

Pretty. Amy frowns at this idea but shrugs it off and takes a sip. "Want to sit outside?"

"Sure." They walk out, and she moves the two chairs around to face each other. Her heart beats faster, feeling exposed with him in her space, with her things.

"What'd you do today?" He raises an eyebrow at her.

"Went on a rum tasting tour, met two cool girls,

then just hung out." She thinks of the laptop and wishes she'd cleared her search history in case he opens it. *Quit being dumb.* Her brows furrow at her insecurity.

As he talks about his day, she half listens as she checks him out. His shirt today says, "Smooth as Tennessee Whiskey." She thinks it's a reference to a country song but can't be sure.

"I thought about you all day today." He reaches for her hand. She takes it and squeezes it.

"Just a sec." She scans the room for her iPad and the small speaker. *Music. I need music.* Shaking slightly, she connects the Bluetooth and chooses a playlist on Spotify. She hates that it's called classic rock. *Classic rock is what my parents listen to.*

A 1980s hair band song blares on the small speaker. *Ha. One of my favorites.* This song makes her lean back in her seat, more comfortable. *Why are you so nervous, anyway? You'll never see him again after this, so just make it fun.* Amy sings every lyric along in her head while he talks about his day, and she paws at the drawstring on her swimsuit cover-up.

She sips the umbrella drink, the syrupy fruitiness what she'd wanted a couple of nights ago. He's so thoughtful. Her gaze shifts to his crotch, and her desire surges. She needs to put her hands on him, but instead, she shifts in her seat and lights a cigarette.

"Nice choice of music."

Amy can't tell if he's being serious or sarcastic, so she ignores the comment.

"I wanted to ask you last night, but you left in a rush. What is that tattoo you have on your shoulder? I was a little preoccupied and didn't really get to see it." He grins, gazing at her shoulder.

Without thinking, she reaches for her right shoulder, almost expecting to feel the thin, light lines of the eagle feather.

"What does it mean to you?" He touches his chest where his bear tattoo is located. She likes that he assumes there's meaning behind it.

"Oh, it's just something my best friend and I got together." She looks away from him so he can't see the flinch in her eyes.

"And why isn't your best friend on this trip with you?"

"Because she's dead." Amy has never been so blunt with these words before. Dead seems so…final. Even saying it out loud, it still feels impossible. She wasn't even forty-three years old. Way too soon. She finishes her rum punch and stares at the red tiles on the floor. She twirls the umbrella in her hands and twists it around in her palm.

"Oh, I'm so sorry."

"Thanks." She doesn't volunteer any other information, and he doesn't ask. She's grateful. He squeezes her leg just above her knee.

Amy asks him about the bear tattoo, and he tells her it was something he got when he was nineteen but regretted soon after. "It's so big, bigger than I expected."

"I know how it is when something is bigger than expected." She winks at him. Sexual innuendos are always a desirable subject change.

He finishes his drink, sets the cup on the small glass table between them, and she goes inside to get them beers. She's pretty sure his gaze bores into her back as she slides her body between the glass doors.

She comes out on the balcony, sets the beers down, and moves toward him. He reaches for her waist and pulls her down, so she sits on his lap. Amy leans in to kiss his neck, and he turns his head to put his lips on her mouth. He nibbles at her bottom lip, teasing. Despite the sunset, it's still hot on the balcony and sweat drips between her breasts and beads on her upper lip. He traces the sweat with his finger between her breasts. One of the best kisses she's ever had. Deep and soft yet full of feeling. Of emotion.

His hardness grows on her thigh, and desire overwhelms her. *I want his fucking cock.* His hardness and hands on her body causes her back to arch.

"I'm going to taste you. Sit still." She moves his arms down to his sides, slides down onto the tile floor, and pulls his legs apart. That wasn't even in the article.

She fingers the button on his cargo shorts and tells him to raise his hips. He complies, gaze not leaving her face. The intensity of his stare sends flutters of need in her pussy, but she ignores the hunger, in an effort to keep control.

The zipper and button on his shorts make a slight thud as they hit the tile balcony floor. Her cover-up slides over her shoulder, exposing her nipple and breast. Anticipation creates goose bumps on her arms.

His stiff prick stands at attention. Amy grabs ice from the rum punch glass, and for a moment, there's worry in his eyes.

"Is this okay?"

"Yes," he mutters. His gaze switches between her face and her exposed breast.

She stands over him and rubs the ice cube on his inner thighs, as he shivers and moans. She moves the cube at a steady pace, like maple syrup flowing from the container. The ice melts on his sweltering skin and glistens in the dusk. She pops the last piece in her mouth. Her mouth, hot for him, is a vast contrast.

He reaches for her nipples, but she pushes his hands down to his sides. She's in control of when and how he touches her.

She removes his shirt, which has become damp from sweat. Amy grabs another piece of ice and stands in front of him. Even before she touches his nipple with the frozen cube, he whimpers. She rubs the ice methodically around each nipple, then down his happy trail and up again until it melts away and he's panting. She teases him, putting the ice near the tip of his cock, but moves it to his pelvis instead. The tip of his cock glistens with pre-cum, and she knows he's hot for her. He needs her. He tries to pull her onto his lap, facing him, but she resists. *I'm in fucking charge.*

"Take two fingers and shove them in my cunt," Amy orders him, sounding more confident than she feels. *Just act like you know what you're doing.* Fake it till you make it. She changes position so he can accommodate her demand.

He obeys.

His fingers enter her in one swoop, and he probes her inside, exploring. But she wants it harder and quicker.

"Faster," she demands in a low voice.

His cadence is in and out, in and out, every so often brushing her clit with his thumb, stimulating desire in every inch of her body.

"*Yes.* Good boy." She sighs. "Good boy" is less cheesy now than when she'd read about it earlier.

She pushes his hands down to his sides because she needs his cock inside her. She straddles him, and in one motion, she bears down, taking his entire length inside her. They both gasp, and she lets the pleasure of being filled by his cock wash over her.

He tries to grab her by the waist, but she puts his hands down, moving her hips in rhythm to the sounds of '80s heavy metal music. She sits on his lap, using her legs for leverage, and pumps up and down on his throbbing dick.

"Oh yes, ride that dick."

"Shut up." Amy quiets him, and he peers at her like a puppy. She's proud of her braveness, for acting in a way she isn't used to, nor totally comfortable with. More confident, she continues.

He sighs when she stops. Control. It's delicious.

She gets off his dick and pulls him to a standing position, grabbing his hand to show they're going inside. She takes the music in with them. His gaze questions her. She sits on the couch and pulls his hand down until he's kneeling in front of her.

"Lick my pussy." She holds his gaze, willing him to do what she wants. He looks away.

He spreads her legs apart to lick her juices mixed with his pre-cum. He flicks his tongue on her clit and moves two fingers inside of her.

"Faster. Deeper."

His flicking and fingering cause Amy's hips to push toward him, raising the intensity. "Put a finger in my ass," she commands, knowing her juices have soaked his fingers enough to be a lubricant.

He submits, fingering both of her holes while making small, fast circles around her clit with his tongue. *Oh God.* He taps her clit with his mouth and sucks it. Every nerve is hot and on fire. Her ass clenches, the desire overwhelming.

The sheer decadence of the moment, she wants to delay her orgasm. The sense of control, of power, is even more sexy than expected. Power is a comfortable feeling in all areas of her life but this one. She had no idea how divine it would be.

A man who will do anything. *Fulfill my desires.* But she can't hold on any longer. She squirts her juices into his mouth and soaks the couch as he continues to finger her. She shrieks as twitches travel down her body, then moves his hand away because the aftershocks are too much. Her spasms are uncontrollable, yet still filled with desire for more.

He stays there on his knees for a few seconds, his panting matching hers. They lock gazes, and he grins. She pulls him from his knees to sit next to her on the couch, straddling him for a second as she scoots to the other side of him to avoid the soaked part of the cushions.

"What was that?" His voice is high and scratchy.

"You've never experienced female squirting before?" She smiles, reserved.

"That was fucking amazing." His dick still stands at attention, reminding her that it's his turn.

"I want to taste your cum." She grabs his hand and pulls him from the couch to bring him into the bedroom. She pulls down the scratchy hotel sheets and sits him down. "Relax."

Amy grabs his cock and slides her hand over it, picking up the pace as his breathing quickens. She puts her mouth around the tip, gripping the shaft and moving her hand at the base of his scrumptious dick. She moves her tongue around the tip of his cock, tasting herself on him. She's delicious. He's delicious. They are delicious together.

"Oh yes," he proclaims.

She moves her hands and takes his whole dick into her mouth, muttering, "Mmm, yeah," as she glides her lips over his cock.

"Can I come?"

"Yes, good boy, you can come in my mouth." The awkwardness of using those words has fallen away.

He shoots his fiery liquid into the back of her throat as his body shudders. It slides down her throat, making her already wet pussy thirst for more. There's no way to avoid being drunk on him.

She moves herself to sit next to him.

"Wow," he whispers through panting.

He wraps his arm around her and scoots closer to her. He makes small circles around her hard nipples.

"I really like you, Amy. You're sexy as fuck, sweet, and smart. It's a trifecta."

Is he just saying that because he has orgasm afterglow?

"I think you're quite the trifecta yourself." Avoiding his gaze and feeling exposed, she grabs her cover-up.

"Where are you going?"

"To pee, then smoke and finish my beer."

"No cuddling? Again?" He grins and follows her.

Cuddling means getting too close, and actually requires she admit she likes him. Maybe that's not such a fucking bad thing.

They sit on the balcony and drink a few more beers

while she smokes. The conversation comes easy as they talk about life at home and his adventures traveling all over the world installing elevators. He talks about his team and gives background on each of them. He's funny and smart. *Don't like him too fucking much.* It's like they've known each other for years. This is just a fun vacation thing. Right? That's all.

"What time do you have to work tomorrow?"

"Seven a.m." He pulls his phone from his cargo shorts, which are still on the balcony. "It's already midnight."

She looks at her phone twice to confirm it's really that late. "Do you want to stay here?"

"Oh, now you want to cuddle," he teases.

"Yeah, kinda." She giggles, feeling close to him and brushing thoughts away about cuddling taking their relationship to the next level. It doesn't have to be like that. *You can just enjoy the comfort of someone sleeping next to you without it requiring a relationship. God, quit overthinking everything.*

She puts her cigarette out, and he follows her into the bedroom. She lies on her side, her favorite sleeping position. He spoons her, and his cock stiffens against her ass. Her nipples harden and brush against the scratchy sheets.

"Wanna?" They both know what he's talking about.

"Yep." Only a moment after her response, he shoves himself into her while they both remain on their sides. He reaches around to explore her clit as he drives himself inside her in a deliberate way. The music is still playing, and he pumps his cock to the rhythm of a song that talks about southern style and slow sex. The lyrics are not lost on her. This lazy, slow pace is nearly as sexy as their faster pace. This has more emotion rather than their earlier animalistic need.

Their hips move together in slow circles, less needy than last night or earlier in the evening. Amy reaches her hand around to touch his bicep, which is tight as he shifts his fingers from her clit to her hips to get leverage. Her hand on him makes her fingers electrified. He pumps into her, hitting deep. As he becomes more aroused and closer to climax, he moves his hand from her waist and paws at her tits, squeezing her hard nipples. Her head spins.

She moves his hand to her clit, and he rubs it, pressing his thumb on it. She closes her eyes hard, for a second, waiting for the inevitable blackness that would soon appear. He takes the cue and pushes his cock further into her pussy, more desperate. Amy's pussy is oozing juices again, and he uses those juices to lubricate his fingers, making quick circles on her clit. Elation fills her body.

"I will soak your cunt with my cum." He is panting for breath and about to lose control.

"Yes, Parker, come in me," she begs, her voice barely perceptible.

He explodes inside her, soaking her. She gasps for air as his nectar seeps out of her. She exuberantly rubs her clit, and he pumps in and out, faster than before. His dick rubs her sweet spot, deep inside, and she bursts with a thunderous moan, no doubt audible down the hallway. She shivers and pushes her sweaty hair out of her face. He leaves his dick inside her and kisses the nape of her neck, sending shudders down her spine again.

Amy turns around to face him. His eyes are closed, and he reaches for her. He finds her waist, puts his arms around her, and they fall asleep taking in each other's breath. She cuddles him. It's been a long time since she's been this safe. And satisfied.

Chapter Ten
Lunch Break

The next morning, she awakens to pee, her footsteps covering the sound of his gentle snoring. She looks at the clock on the nightstand. Seven thirty a.m. Music still blares from the speaker.

"Shit! Parker. You're late."

His confused eyes open, and he looks at the clock. "Shit." He flies out of bed, finds his shorts and shirt still on the balcony, and throws them on. Amy stands by the open door, and he brushes her lips with his in a hasty goodbye, door slamming behind him.

Naked, she stands there for a second, glancing at the still-wet spot on the couch. A butterfly flutters deep within her, from already missing his presence.

She climbs into bed and falls into a dreamless sleep.

She wakes in a fetal position and reaches for the other side of the bed. He's gone. The clock shows eleven forty-nine a.m., and she does a double take to make sure she saw it right.

Dragging herself to the phone, she's already in the routine of ordering room-service coffee. This time, she orders a full American breakfast, complete with sausage, eggs, and toast. Breakfast comes, and she eats on the balcony, the plate hot on her lap. The rum punch cup is still there, pale from melted ice and sun.

She sips coffee and considers what she wants to do today. *If I don't come back with a tan, people will wonder what I did on vacation.* She smiles to herself, devilishly. Amy decides she'll go to the pool. After a scorching hot shower and a bath in sunscreen, she heads down.

When the server asks her what she wants, she starts to ask for a mimosa, then decides water is the better choice. *I've been drinking a lot.* Instead of reading, she brought her iPad down to play games, *Candy Crush* being one of her favorites.

Amy slides into the pool, a welcome relief from the relentless sun, putting her large-brimmed hat on to keep the sun off her face. She sits on the pool stairs and notices the couple she saw fighting a few days ago. They glare at each other as they sit side by side on lounge chairs a few down from hers. She moves through water toward them, looking at something else, so she can hear what they're saying.

"You're the one ruining this vacation. Do you know how much I paid to take you somewhere nice? The least you could do is appreciate it." The bearded man in his twenties has fire in his eyes.

"I contribute too, so you weren't the only one that paid for this. Besides, what's the big deal about wanting to sleep in on vacation?" She looks away from him.

"The problem is you're lazy. You sleep in at home, and I wanted to do another tour today."

Amy can't look away. Her nostrils flare at the similarities between this guy and her ex-husband. Vacations with him always included sweaty, hot hikes, bike rides, and tours. No sleeping in or just relaxing by the pool was allowed.

She's desperate to tell the woman she can do whatever she wants on vacation.

"Lazy? I work sixty hours a week in that shitty hospital." The pretty woman tucks her pixie haircut behind her ears and shoots lasers in his direction.

"Yeah, all the while you leave me at home to fend for myself." His gaze narrows.

"Fine, we can go on the tour tomorrow. Which one is the most interesting to you?" She picks up a brochure and hands it to him.

Tears well, again. She wonders how many times she and her ex-husband had the same exact conversation. It always went down the same way. He'd blame her for something, tell her she'd hurt his feelings, then insult her. When she'd defend herself, he'd play the victim. Then she'd try to hug him and apologize so they wouldn't fight. This interaction put her relationship with her ex-husband in a new light. She's grateful for this, yet sad for the pretty, pixie-haircut woman.

Fucking asshole. She understands how alone the woman must feel.

She shakes her head to lose the thought and turns to the vision of Parker's muscular arms holding her all night. Safety. Comfort. Katy once told her, years ago, "You light up every room you enter." This was an attempt to counterattack any self-esteem ruining her ex-husband had done. At the time, she scoffed at Katy's comment, but maybe, just maybe, she was right. Parker's voice whispers behind her, and she jumps.

"Hey, pretty lady."

She turns and smiles at him. He's in his work clothes, and he waves at her, his hands greasy from work. *So hot.*

"Well, hi." *Dumb response.* Where was the wittiness she showed in her classroom?

"Whatcha doing?"

"Oh, you know, just killing it at *Candy Crush* and soaking in the sun. I have just four more nights here and figure I better get a tan."

He grins at her, his eyes glowing. "Want to go to my room? I'm on a half-hour break."

"Yes, please." She leaves her things.

She slips on her cover-up. The aroma of sex from last night, still on the fabric, rises to tickle her nose. He waits for her at the edge of the pool and takes her hand. She grabs it without thinking as they make their way to his room.

"I've been thinking about you all day."

"I've been thinking about you too," Amy stutters like a nervous schoolgirl. The flowery shadows on the stucco walls dance in the sunshine as they make their way down the hallway. As soon as they're out of sight, he forces his hips forward to push her against the wall and cups her chin, brings her lips to his. She exhales into the kiss, and her thighs clench.

He cups her breasts and moves his hands down her rib cage, to her ass, then to the top of her chest. They release lips to take a breath, and he says, "I need you." He pulls her by the hand again toward his room.

His hands shake as he uses the room key to open the door. Once inside, he moves her to the bed and lays her down, sliding off her hot-pink swimsuit bottoms. She catches a glimpse of his strong hands, hands that have already given her so much pleasure, and involuntary wetness seeps onto the bed. *Men who work with their hands are hot as fuck.* She opens her legs, and while eyeing her cunt, he drops his work pants, and the belt buckle thuds against the floor. His freed dick pops up. He licks his lips and spits into his hand, driving his fingers into her. Satisfied she is wet enough, he grunts, leans over her, and grabs his cock to push himself inside of her. She yelps with desire at being filled with him again so soon. She believes she'll never be able to get enough of him. Ever.

He pushes into her. "Turn around." He grabs her by the waist and helps her. "Put your ass in the air. Higher."

On all fours, she uses all her strength to hold herself in place as he grunts and thrusts into her, becoming more urgent. "I've been thinking about fucking you again all morning," he mutters into her ear. His breath is fiery, and her panting is more intense as his speed increases. She's happy to give him this pleasure.

"Oh yes, baby, I'm so close. Do you want me to come in you?"

"Yes, please." Her voice is hoarse. While he catches his breath, he pumps in a steady motion into her, draining his dick. The hotness of his load envelops her from the inside. Some of his cum squeezes out between his dick and her pussy, dripping onto the bed.

"Your turn." Parker flips her around onto her back. He spreads her legs, kneels on the bed in front of her, and leans in to lick her cum-filled pussy. She loves the thought of him licking his cum out of her, as if they are one person. She holds his gaze, showing him her pleasure. He paddles her G-spot, his tongue alternating between quick and hard licks. His dick glistens in sunlight from his cum and her juices.

Amy raises her hips, pushing them against his mouth until she's close to bursting. The heat rises from her toes to her head.

"Yes, baby, come for me." He knows she's close.

Her excitement wafts through room. She welcomes the blackness and screams as shivers envelop her body. He continues to lick her slower now, then allows the orgasm to settle before he stops. She opens her eyes, and he's smiling at her.

"This was way better than a burger." He stands and grabs his work pants off the floor. Amy looks at the clock; he has just ten more minutes of break, and the walk to the resort must be at least that long. She isn't offended because she understands he has to get to work.

She puts on her damp swimsuit bottoms, and he strides over to her, grabs her by the chin, and kisses her lips, leaving the taste of her pussy on her mouth.

"Hey, so I have virtual work meetings tonight so we can wrap up this project with the regional manager, and I'm pretty tired already—you did keep me up late last night. So I can't get together tonight. But can I take you to dinner tomorrow night?"

Oooh, a date. I knew I fucking liked this guy. Her eyes open wide. "Sure. What time?"

"Does seven work?"

"Let me check my schedule." Amy pretends to look at a fake calendar.

"Great, seven it is. I can't wait to see you again."

"Me either."

With that, they both leave his room, her to her lounge chair, him, to work.

Chapter Eleven
Sister's Advice

The rest of Amy's afternoon is unremarkable except for the flush on her face. Napping, people watching, playing her game. Fucking perfect day. When the sun sets, her steps are slow and tentative because soreness in her pussy has set in. The song "Hurts so Good" repeats itself over and over in her mind.

After arriving in her room, she takes a long shower, letting the hot water run over her body. She puts on a robe and sits on the balcony with a bottle of water and her pack of cigarettes. Music. *I need background music.* She gets her speaker and iPad, and puts on Tom Petty. Sighing, her computer calls. Fucking technology. Her lips turn into a smile when she reads an email from a student thanking her for an amazing class and saying she wants to become a professor, too. That made checking emails worth it.

Two hours later, she's weary from being transported to her regular work-life. She slams her computer shut and takes a beer from the overstocked mini fridge. The tip for housekeeping worked.

She doesn't remember a time where she has been so disconnected from her phone—and control over her work-life and hunts around the room for it. She checks, and there are seventy-seven text messages. Amy sighs and goes through them. Most of them are from a group text she's in with her girlfriends.

Her laugh echoes at the sarcastic memes her friends have been sending to each other. Those ladies are what's kept her sane over the last year. She sends them a selfie she took at the pool earlier. The sarcastic duck face she was making was sure to get a laugh from those girls.

Amy finds Jennifer's number, the woman she met rum tasting, and texts her.

—*What are you up to?*—

—*Having dinner. We partied too hard last night and are going to stay at our hotel tonight and go to bed early.*—

Damn. She'd have liked to drink with them tonight.

—*Totally understand. What are you doing tomorrow?*—

—*We have an all-day snorkeling tour and a dinner cruise. Want to meet up night after next and party with us? We are going to Bambu, a nightclub on the harbor.*—

—*That sounds great. Let's do it. Have fun snorkeling.*—

Loneliness creeps in.

Amy switches the music to an eighties hair band rock station. There's something about this music that makes her feel comforted and less alone. She sips her beer and watches people below. There's a couple sitting close together on a concrete bench and laughing. Amy watches them and wonders if they're as happy as they look.

When she was with her ex-husband, she's sure there must have been moments like that. When she had married him, she thought he checked all the boxes—

good job, stable income, handsome, and attentive. Turns out it requires more to be happy, and people change. *At least I learned that in my fucking forties.*

The morose place she was going is changed by images of Parker's smile. They've talked for hours, and his intensity and enthusiasm to know everything about her was almost better than the sex. *Parker, fucking get out of my head.* This is just a fling, nothing more. They live two thousand miles apart. This will be nothing more than what it is, a good time with no attachment.

Her phone lights up, creating a needed distraction. It's a text from her sister.

—Hey sis. How's your trip? Please tell me you aren't working too much.—

—It's amazing. I met two cool girls yesterday and hung out by the pool today. And funny you mention work, I just shut my laptop.—

—Stop working. You are on vacation. Sis you don't always have to be the perfect employee you know. You could use some of that obsessive compulsiveness for other things—

—I met a guy.—

—Okay I'll bite tell me about him.—

She tells her sister about Parker. Since her sister is a bit of a prude, she leaves out all the great sex and gives her the romantic details she knows her sister will love—meeting in the elevator, the cute crossbody bag he left on her chair, and the dinner date they have tomorrow.

—Did you, you know…—

She hates that her sister knows her so well. Despite her married dry spell, Ava remembers all too well the parade of boyfriends Amy had prior to meeting her ex-husband. Those boyfriends somehow were easy to let go to avoid letting them have control. As soon as she sensed the least amount of control or jealousy, she'd break up with them. She's not sure what changed with her ex-husband. Her life would have been different if she'd let him go much sooner. Never mind that, that's old news now, though.

She sends Ava a devil face.

—I knew it. You've been so quiet via text, I figured something distracted you. I thought you went on that trip to sort through feelings about all the shit you've endured over the past year. Do I have to list it out for you? Maybe you should take it easy on the romance.—

When Amy doesn't answer, Ava continues.

—Listen everyone knows your ex was an idiot. You need time to figure out how you will get over the emotionally abusive narcissistic jerk. Perhaps jumping in bed with someone else isn't the right way to do that—

Ava always tries to mother her.

—I'm good. It is just fun; I'm not getting attached. I'm not overthinking it.—

—Are you sure?—

—Yep.—

Amy sends a smiley face and changes the subject again.

—How are Keegan and Kayla? And Mom and Dad?—

Her niece and nephew are like the kids Amy never had. She savors every moment she has with them.

—I see what you did there. They're all doing good. Mom took a fall yesterday but she's fine.—

—Shit, Mom's okay, then? Any word from Kyle?—

Kyle, Ava's cheating husband, unlike her own ex-husband, changed only during the last couple years of marriage. It's a mystery why Ava gets defensive when she talks bad about him.

—Yeah, they're fine. Kyle asked me to go to coffee and told me he misses me.—

—You said no, right?—

A pang of guilt sends a shiver into Amy's stomach. She cheated on her ex-husband with Kevin. Although her ex-husband never found out, she knows firsthand the impact cheating created on Ava's psyche.

—We are co-parenting so we need to talk.—

—Mmm hmmm.—

The texts from Ava stop. She knows she's hit a nerve, so she changes the subject again.

—How are things at the hospital?—

—Good, busy. We installed a new IT system, so I've been training everyone on it. Sorta fun.—

—That sounds exciting. I'm going to order room service for dinner. Chat soon?—

—Sure. I love you, Sis.—

—I love you too. Goodnight.—

Her stomach growls. Very used to takeout in her busy life at home, she calls room service and orders all her favorite things, not caring about the cost nor the calories—a bottle of Malbec wine, mozzarella sticks, salad, steak, a baked potato, and for dessert, chocolate cake.

While waiting for room service, Amy pulls out her iPad to play *Candy Crush* and settles on the balcony. She has depleted all her lives in the game when the food comes. The server sets the table, the crisp white tablecloth matching the napkin he placed under the silverware. He opens the bottle of wine and pours her a glass. It seems he will never leave so she can dive into the steamy plates of food.

As she takes slow bites of everything, she wonders about the potential of truth in what Ava said. *Was my ex really an abuser? A narcissist?* The argument at the pool was one that hit close to home, and that's how she'd peg that guy. *For someone who's supposed to be smart, it sure took you long enough to fucking pick up on that.*

For the first time in a long time, when she thinks about her divorce, she smiles instead of being sad. A bullet was dodged. A lot more time may have been wasted, but it wasn't. She raises her glass into the air, toasting freedom.

Amy finds her laptop, opens it, and googles "professor jobs in Nashville, Tennessee." *Maybe I could move there?* A few postings appear for professor jobs at Vanderbilt University and Belmont University, and she's halfway through reading them, then slams the computer shut. *What the fuck are you doing?* This is just a vacation fling, nothing more. Is it the right time to get serious with someone? Be vulnerable? Of course, that's assuming he wants something serious. Which he may not.

She considers her options, given the direction her feelings are going for Parker. *Is Ava right? Should I just focus on healing from the events of the last year? Fuck it. He's only here for two more days. I'll just keep an emotional distance.* Amy takes a huge bite of chocolate cake and smiles. *Yeah, that's what I'll do.*

After eating, she finds her favorite movie, a 1980s movie where kids are stuck in detention on a Saturday.

She mouths the lines by heart, eyes heavy. Unable to fight sleep, her dreams are nonspecific but include visions of Parker. They clasp each other's hands in her dream and are somewhere foreign.

Chapter Twelve
The Casino

She can't stop grinning at the thought of her date tonight with Parker. Despite an early morning sunrise walk to calm her nerves, she still paces around her room. It will be her first date since before she got married. With Kevin, they had to sneak around and were just able to meet at his house or at motels. With Alejandro, they just saw each other on the boat. The anticipation makes it difficult for her to focus on the day.

As a distraction, Amy opens her laptop to check emails. As often happens, one task leads to another, and she works most of the day. Her persistent thoughts turn to Parker's smile, his laugh, his face, and she dismisses them so she can focus. *Ugh, work again. It's okay because I'm sitting on the balcony in the sun. Way different from working at home.* A therapist once told her she works so much so that she doesn't have to deal with emotions like anger and disappointment. Defensive, she had responded with, "I work too much because I want to be successful." Judgmental and knowing, the therapist had responded with, "Have you ever thought about why you're so driven to be, what you call, successful?" Despite this, she works until almost five p.m.

Dripping wet after a shower, she rifles through the

clothes in the hotel closet for something to wear. She tries on four different dresses, then settles on a strapless black-and-white dress, the flower print barely noticeable unless you look closely. No underwear, of course. She stares at the wedge heels, shifting her weight from leg to leg, undecided.

Will it seem like I am trying too hard? She puts them on anyway and likes the way they make her legs look. *I feel fucking sexy.*

Well, sexy for a forty-something-year-old woman. She takes several steps to make sure she can walk in them. She balances on the heels in front of the mirror and curls her long hair. She frowns when some curls become kinked. The black eyeliner and mascara and finishing touch—red lipstick—make her look put together. She's satisfied.

Shit. Five forty-five. Now what? *I have over an hour to wait.*

Amy grabs the bottle of wine she didn't finish last night, pours a glass of the deep red liquid, and takes it on the balcony where her cigarettes are. Just as she's about to snuff out a cigarette, she jumps when the hotel room phone rings.

She runs in to answer.

"Hey, you." Parker's sexy Southern drawl makes her swoon.

"Hey."

"So I got off work early. I was wondering if you'd like to go have dinner earlier than what we planned?

"Sure."

"Great, I will jump in the shower, then I'll pick you up in your room." Old-fashioned. *Picking me up.* Love it.

"Perfect." Amy twirls her hair around her fingers and hangs up the phone. She alternates pacing in her room, taking a large swallow of wine every time she paces by the table.

Fifteen minutes later, a light tap causes her to lose grip on the wine glass, almost causing a spill. She stands too quickly, blood rushing to her head, and her ankle rolls in the heels. *Fuck.* She straightens her dress and ignores the throbbing in her ankle.

When she opens the door, he says nothing just looks her up and down.

He whistles between his teeth. "You are gorgeous."

"Thank you." She looks away from his gaze.

His polo shirt hugs his arms. Her gaze drifts over the rest of his outfit, resting for a second on the delicious outline of his package in the flat front slacks. Longing wells in her, but she resists the urge to claw at the bear tattoo on his chest and tell him, *fuck dinner.*

"You look great yourself. Come in for a pre-dinner drink?"

"You mean a pre-funk?" He grins at her.

"Yes. Exactly." She laughs because that's what her and her friends call drinking before going to the "main event."

Parker reaches for her waist and plants a long, soft kiss on her lips. "Is it weird to say I missed you? I hardly know you, but I thought about you all day."

Amy smiles at him but doesn't answer. *I know the feeling.* She grabs two beers from the fridge, and they settle on the balcony. He fills her in on his day, and she tells him about her uneventful time working.

After finishing their beers, they head out to catch a taxi. She takes baby steps and wobbles in her heels. He takes her arm.

"The Atlantis on Paradise Island," he tells the cab driver. She's excited. She's heard about this huge casino hotel in Nassau but has never been there. In fact, it was on her list of places to go while in Nassau. The butterflies have subsided after their chat on the balcony—and the beer didn't hurt either.

"I hope you like steak?"

"I do." Amy's mouth waters as she thinks of the mediocre, lukewarm steak she had last night.

"Perfect." He puts his hand on her knee, brushing his fingertips up to her inner thigh. She grins at him. His hand finds her pussy. He makes small circles around the outside of her lips, causing a position shift to accommodate the moistness. Grinning, she remembers all the conversations her and her friends have had regarding the word "moist." People have strong feelings about the word, and to tease her friends, she'd sent "moist" memes all week to her girlfriends just to annoy them. She spreads her legs apart a little more.

She glances at the taxi driver, wondering if he can see Parker's hand up her dress. Surprising herself, she wishes he can. What's that called again? Yes, that's right. Voyeurism. She moans low, hoping the taxi driver can hear, sending shivers down her own spine. He continues tickling and tempting her pussy and inserts a finger, when the cab driver announces, "We're here," breaking the spell. He sits in the back seat for a moment and grabs her arm, so she faces him. He licks the finger that was inside her and mouths, *Yum*. Her heart skips a beat. She glances at the rearview mirror and sees the taxi driver wink. She clenches.

Her wedge heel shoes *click-clack* on the marble tile

when they enter the lobby. She brushes her hand over the columns, to feel the coolness of the stone. Her gaze follows the column to the ceiling, where hundreds of mosaic tiles dance in the light. Squinting, she sees the shape of sea creatures, an octopus at the center. He appears as if he is starting down at her, and she stands still, looking in awe. The sea creatures bring memories of scuba diving—something she hasn't done enough lately. The vague sound of slot machines makes her smile, as it reminds her of amazing times in Las Vegas with her girlfriends.

Parker reaches for her hand while they look at the hotel map to determine where the restaurant is located. She squeezes his hand. He squeezes, her fingers snug in his large hands.

They walk for fifteen minutes to find Seafire Steakhouse. When they sit at a cozy table in the corner, Amy opens the menu, her mouth waters again. *Holy shit, this place is expensive. I guess elevator installers make more money than I assumed.* This is a surprising thought to her because when she got married, she assumed the businessman types, like her ex-husband, were the only ones that could afford to take her to fancy restaurants. This of course doesn't mean she can't afford to buy herself a nice dinner, but who doesn't like to be treated like a lady? Even if that notion is old-fashioned.

They share a shellfish tower for two as an appetizer, and both order the rib eye steaks for dinner along with two sides—mashed potatoes and mac and cheese. *Fuck yeah, let's carb out.* He orders a bottle of wine from Washington and swirls it around and sips like you're supposed to. Amy's lower region tickles.

Wow. Great in bed, and also has wine tasting manners.

She remembers he told her he has a daughter, so she asks him about her. She wants to know everything from his perspective about having a child, like his reaction when he found out they were pregnant and his experiences with her as a baby. She likes the way his eyes light up when talks about his kid.

"It's been hard to be without my baby girl since we got divorced."

Amy nods, trying to understand it from the perspective of losing her dog to her ex, even though she knows this isn't anywhere near the same.

The bottle is empty before they finish their appetizer, and he orders another. She picks at her food.

"Fucking eat." He stabs an entire shrimp with his fork and puts it all in his mouth. *Fuck it.* She shovels in food, perhaps a bit more ladylike than when she was alone in her room last night—but not much more.

She tells him about living in Washington and all the wineries there are to visit. She tells him of a time she and Katy spent a long weekend in Walla Walla and went to every winery the town offers. She laughs when she tells him about how drunk they were by the end of the day. The snobby winemaker asked them to leave because they were being too loud and rowdy. They giggled all the way back and ordered room service, enough for six. They ate on the bed, food and crumbs dripping everywhere on the scratchy brown seventies bedspread while listening to '80s new wave music. The band reminded them of years past when they'd worn black lipstick and dressed in all black. It was the first time Amy told a story about Katy without having to shove down tears.

"You miss her, don't you?" He tilts his head and bores his gaze into her. Luckily, their entrees arrive; an easy way to change the subject. *For once, I want to talk about it, though. I want him to know everything.* After they finish the delicious meal, he scoots around the table, so he's sitting next to her. He whispers, "I want you for dessert."

"But all in good time." He smiles. They order cheesecake and chocolate cake—her favorite—for dessert. As they linger over the last of their wine, he asks if she'd like to go into the casino.

"Sure, I'm not much of a gambler, but it sounds fun."

Parker pays the check. He links his arm with hers; the wine causes her head to spin, in a delicious, new way. This is a date. This is the exact definition of a date.

They walk around the casino, and Parker explains the game of craps to her.

"It still makes no sense," she admits.

He plays alone, and she stands beside him, proud to be on his arm. When he loses three times in a row, he whispers, "I don't need good luck. I already had my good fortune meeting you."

Her cheeks flush, his words making her radiate pleasure from her toes to her head. *It's just a fling,* she reminds herself.

"Want to get a drink and then maybe head back?" He winks. Her thighs clench.

"Absolutely." And they settle into seats at a place called the Moon Bar. The lights on the enormous chandelier around the square bar change from purple to blue. The bar also has a gigantic fish tank, and they watch the jellyfish move in the water while sipping their red wine. The chatter of people drowns out the hip hop music the bar plays.

Amy looks around at the other patrons and notices the bartender from her hotel, Jaden, sitting at the bar across from them. She smiles and waves.

Parker follows her gaze to see where she's looking and waves too. Parker motions for Jaden to come over. Jaden grabs his drink and walks over to them.

"Hey, man, I almost didn't recognize you out of your element."

Jaden is wearing tight black skinny jeans and a fitted button-up shirt. *Pretty trendy for a guy in his fifties.* Very cute, she decides.

"Want to join us?"

"Sure." Jaden sets his drink down next to her.

Parker and Jaden make small talk. Zoning out on happy tingles, she nods and smiles at the right times, pretending like she isn't considering something more with Parker.

Amy asks Jaden about living on the island. She apologizes because everyone probably asks him these questions. Every few seconds, Jaden looks around the bar, focusing on the entrance.

"Are you waiting for someone?" She cocks her head at Jaden.

"Yes." His gaze casts downward to the floor. "A Tinder date."

His phone beeps. His lips turn downward at the corner when he reads the message.

"She can't make it and wants to reschedule."

Poor guy.

"You can hang with us." He glances sideways at

Amy to make sure it's okay.

Amy orders a round of Lick My Pussy shots, containing coconut rum and pineapple juice. This is a shot she and Katy used to order when they were single in their awkward attempts to flirt with men. It was always funny when a guy said, "Can I buy you a drink?" And she answered, "Sure, Lick My Pussy."

They have two more drinks when Parker squeezes her hand. She squeezes twice. *We already have a secret language.* Warmth moves from her toes to her head.

"We're going to take off." Parker pats Jaden's shoulder.

"Okay, I'll stay a while and drown my sorrows even more." He gives them a half smile.

Before the driver has even put the car into gear, Parker's hand is on her inner thigh. Her cunt gets wet—*moist*—and shivers move from the bottom of her spine to the top, then down again. She shudders and welcomes the igniting flame buried deep inside of her.

When they arrive at the hotel, Parker pulls her toward his room. She takes her wedges off, a bit grossed out by her bare feet on the hallway floor. The blister on her heel throbs. *Fucking heels.*

A gasp is audible when she takes in his transformed room.

There has to be over a hundred candles maybe more lit around the room, on the bedside tables, desk, and on the floor. They light the rose petals scattered everywhere. Her mouth drops open, she looks at him, questioning. Happiness overtakes her. Maybe this isn't just a fling. Why go to so much trouble if it were?

"Since I've been here so long, I kind of know the housekeepers. They helped me."

"Thank you, this is beautiful. But you know you don't have to woo me anymore, right? You're getting laid for sure anyway."

"I'll always do everything I can to woo you, sweetheart." His eyes crinkle. *Sweetheart.*

Amy picks up a rose petal and sniffs it, inhaling the sweet scent.

He reaches into the mini fridge, grabs two beers, and he gestures for Amy to sit on the bed, since there is nowhere else to sit. The rose petals *swoosh* as they slide on the duvet cover. Parker turns on country music. *This music may grow on me.* It's more lighthearted. He tells her that during his time working there, he's gotten to know Jaden pretty well—and Jaden has had a string of terrible luck with women. She sips her beer. They don't talk about the fact he's leaving tomorrow.

"I want to give you a massage." He raises his eyebrows and places his beer on the nightstand.

"I'll never say no to a massage." Amy puts her half-drunk beer on the nightstand and reaches and pulls back the scratchy bedspread. Some rose petals get in between the sheets. She worries they will stain but scoffs at the idea, that's what bleach is for.

Parker jumps up and runs into the bathroom. He calls, "Get naked." *Gladly.*

She pulls off her dress, leaving it in a heap next to her wedges. She promises herself to never wear those shoes again and rubs the blister on her heel.

He comes out of the bathroom, carrying one of the mini-size lotions the hotel provides. "Let's start with you on your stomach." The glow of candlelight dances on the walls, and Amy smiles into the pillow. *When was the last time anyone had given her a massage?* She can't remember.

His weight crushes the rose petals, and he reaches for her.

He squeezes the bottle. It makes a *poof* as lotion squirts into his hands. He rubs the lotion, covering his palms, and begins rubbing her. She moans, soft sounds emitting from her parted lips as he rubs her neck, shoulders, and runs his fingers lightly on her spine like a spider. He grabs another handful of lotion, and the scent of lavender and candle wax fills her nose. She squeezes her eyes shut, more contented than she's been in a long time.

He moves his hands down her ample butt. He leans into her ear. "You've got one beautiful ass."

She raises her hips, sticking them out so he can gaze at her luscious backside.

He moves his hands around her butt, her thighs, then her feet. Her entire body is on fire from his lotion filled hands.

"Turn over."

Dizzy from his massaging hands, she turns around. He pulls the sheets back to expose the front of her body.

He whistles, then runs a single finger around each of her nipples, between her breasts, and to her neck. Cupping a breast in each hand, he rubs them both and works his way down to her legs. She shudders when his fingers reach where her thigh and pussy meet.

He moves his hands down her thighs and reaches her feet. He takes her feet in his hands and rubs each toe, resting his thumb and forefinger on the ball of her foot, kneading. She moans. Foot massages are her favorite.

When he's finished, he strokes her hair. "Do you

want to jump in the shower with me?"

Every nerve is on fire from the massage, and she's unclear if it's because of her loose muscles or her growing need to have his hands in every crevice of her body.

She doesn't answer, but instead slithers off the bed, her legs wobbly from the massage.

Parker turns on the shower, and she watches him undress. He pulls off his socks, then grabs the back of his shirt to pull it off without turning it inside out. His gaze not leaving her face, he unbuttons his pants, and they drop in a heap on the bathroom floor. His thick prick stands at attention.

He takes a step back. "You sure are sexy."

"So are you." Amy isn't sure if she's ever been this attracted to someone physically and mentally.

"Let's jump in."

He follows her to the shower. The water is scorching hot, just how she likes it. She wets her hair, then turns to face him. Parker uses the soap to first wash her chest, building a slick lather. He runs the soap down her arms to her pussy, brushing her pussy lips with his fingers. Every delicate touch makes her greedy and inhale deep. The sensual touch and the hot water cause her nipples to harden. The soap still in his hand, he cups each breast, tracing the shape of them with his fingers. Then he bends down and washes her legs, running his hand to where her pussy meets her thigh. He traces the outside of her pussy with his fingers ever so slight. Goose bumps appear on her arms. *Put your fingers in there. Please.* She begs to herself.

"Oh please."

"Not just yet, my sweet. I want to touch every inch

of you." His voice is strong despite the water crashing around them, falling on the tile.

His fingers rest on the outside of her wetness, unmoving. Her mouth opens in protest, a sigh of frustration escaping from her lips.

He follows the outline of her curves, clasps his hand around her waist, and reaches around for more soap lather. He pulls her close and uses his knuckles to rub her spine and shoulder blades with the lather. Her nipples are taut against his chest. When he finishes, he grabs her by the waist and nudges her against the shower wall. He lathers more soap and cups each breast in one hand, flicking her nipples. She shudders. He moves his hands down her belly, tracing the "V" curve of her pussy. Then he grabs the shampoo.

He puts a glob of shampoo in his hand. "Is this okay?"

"Yessss." She's breathless from his slow, erotic, gentle touches. The touches of a boyfriend. Not the touches of a convenient, vacation fuck. She surrenders to his gentleness.

He turns her around and massages shampoo into her scalp before running it down to the ends of her hair. When he's done, he grabs her by the waist to put her under the water to rinse. He holds his hand on her forehead, blocking her eyes from the shampoo and water. Is this guy for fucking real?

He opens the shower and reaches around on the counter for something. It's a razor. "May I?"

"Sure," Amy pants. *Sexy.* This is a first. He grabs her leg, bending it so it's resting on top of his.

He lathers her right leg from her calf to thigh, then runs the razor from her ankle to her upper thigh, and then does the other leg. When he's done with each leg, he sets them down, patting each of them. The intimacy of the moment makes her shudder with a deep emotional yet physical pleasure. And a little bit of fear. Is he too good to be true?

She grabs the soap. "May I?" she repeats his earlier words because they sound, so, well, sweet.

"Yes." He's also breathing heavy.

Amy takes the soap and starts at his chest, washing the mass of hair around his nipples, then down to his dick. Then she lathers her hands and rubs them down his arm, turned on by his bear tattoo. Next, she takes her hand that still holds the soap, grips her hands around his thick cock, teasing him with a soft touch and a slow pace. He moans, and he leans his full weight against the shower wall. Her stroking becomes furious, and he puts his hand over hers to slow her down.

She looks at him with raised eyebrows.

"I'd like for us to take our time tonight."

"Yes." She is fully enveloped in the intimacy of the moment. He guides her hand to squeeze his balls. She kneels and takes his cock in her mouth and tastes his pre-cum on the tip. He moans, and she licks her lips. She explores his wet dick with her mouth, taking her time, before lathering her hands again and massaging the soap into his thighs, down to his feet.

She needs him inside of her now. Right now. To push things along, she gestures to the shower handle. "Are we almost done?"

He doesn't answer her but brushes his lips against hers instead. As the scorching water rushes over them, he reaches around and takes her ass in his hands and seems to draw circles with his fingertips. His mouth opens, and his tongue explores her mouth. The heat from his kiss and the heat of the shower make her flush, every nerve on fire.

"You ready?" Parker reaches for the water handle.

"Sure." She gets out first, pats her body dry, rubs her hair with a towel.

She leaps toward him, takes the towel from him, and dries him off. She starts at his feet and works her way to his muscular calves and thighs, then to this dick, which is still hard. She spends extra time drying him there. Then she moves up to his chest, arms, patting every inch of his body and then his face. When she dries his neck, she can't help but stand on her tiptoes and kiss him just behind the ear, which causes him to shudder.

"You already know my spot, don't you?"

"And you know all of mine."

Parker pulls her to the bed and lays her down.

He spreads her legs apart and rubs tiny circles around her pussy. She opens further to him. The candles create a silhouette of his body on the wall. The new, familiar anticipation of him entering her still and will always command longing.

Parker mounts her, easing himself, little by little, into her drenched pussy. The eagerness of him filling her sets every nerve on fire.

His eyes are open, and he holds her gaze while moving slowly inside of her. The music is still playing, and the lyrics croon about just letting things be and not stressing too much about them in the moment. Amy thinks she's heard this song. How appropriate for this moment.

Parker stops fucking her and mutters, "I need to

taste you, and I want to make you come with my mouth." He lies on his stomach with her legs spread wide and pushes his tongue inside her swollen cunt. His tongue flicks on her clit, and his fingers explore her from the inside.

This motion causes ripples of pure desire and need through her body.

Unable to contain herself any longer, she grabs a handful of sheets and grips the bed. "Oh *yes*," she pants. She craves this orgasm. She wants his mouth and his dick and his fingers clutching her and needing her. His relentless tongue flicking is too much to bear, so she doesn't hold back. The room spins and then goes black. The orgasm lasts for what seems like several minutes. Parker keeps flicking her clit, causing spasms down her spine.

His breath is hot when he kisses her belly, breasts, and neck. Parker finds her lips, and Amy reaches down to put his dick inside her. He gasps when he enters her, and she shudders, still sensitive after the orgasm. He lays flat on top of her, kissing her mouth while he pumps into her to the slow, rhythmic beat of the music.

"Oh my God, I'm going to come." He moans and explodes inside of her. His cum is hot and sticky, and judging by how much wetter her pussy is, it's like a dam exploded inside of her. Perhaps the most satisfied she's ever been.

His hot breath on her neck causes a new longing in her heart and in her mind.

"That was amazing." He slides off her, lying on his side. His dick presses against her hip and continues to throb. He puts an arm around her.

"Indeed." The candle wax swishes in their

containers, from the movement of the bed, and they drip like a whisper onto the floor. The candle wax is a reminder of the time she went to church—the first time in a long time—praying for Katy to magically heal. While she prayed, the lit candle wax dripped onto the floor. She also prayed for God to forgive her for cheating. Drip, drip, drip. Although there was no resolution on that day, the answer seems to be coming to her more and more. In the form of her quiet acceptance of herself. And her mistakes.

They lie there, silent, both deep in thought. She breaks the spell by getting up to pee. He sits next to her on the balcony, hands her a water, and they talk in low whispers. When they go inside, they sit cross-legged on the bed, facing each other.

"Tell me about Katy. It seems to be something on your mind that causes you to drift into a different world and look sad. I can only assume it's because of her."

Amy looks at him, takes a deep breath, and tells him everything without stopping, and avoids guarding and choosing her words like she always does. Just like she did with the therapist. *What can it hurt? I won't see him after he leaves tomorrow anyway. This doesn't make me vulnerable to him.* She lies to herself.

"I signed my divorce papers right before I booked this trip. The divorce was a long and painful process because my ex-husband wanted to fight me on everything. He didn't want the divorce, but I couldn't live that way anymore. The bottom line is he didn't treat me well. I thought he did, but the more I looked at myself from the outside, and how other people saw us, I knew he wasn't good for me. It was scary because I'd put all my eggs in one basket with him. I really thought, when we got married, it'd be forever. Even though I'm the one that wanted the divorce, everything I knew came crashing down. I lost mutual friends, my dog, and everything I knew. I moved from a nice house to a condo. My entire life, as I knew it, was gone. Well, except for my work. Which was probably the only thing that kept me going." She avoids eye contact with him as she blurts this out—the longest run-on sentence ever.

Parker nods every so often and grabs her hand.

"The thing is part of the reason I wanted to leave is that I'd cheated on him and couldn't handle the guilt that brought. I didn't want to live like that—sneaking around all the time. Plus, even though he was an ass, it wasn't fair to him. The guilt ate at me, to where I couldn't focus on anything. I tried pretending like it was justified because he was such an ass."

She pauses and catches his gaze to see his reaction to her indiscretion. He doesn't react, so she goes on. "Anyway, he's a narcissistic asshole, and I'm glad I left. It hasn't been easy, though. I will say, throughout all this, my sister and three close girlfriends have remained on my side, always cheering me on. For that I feel lucky."

He holds her hand tighter, squeezes it. "You've been through a lot. I think you need to figure out how to let go of the guilt, though. You're right, it'll eat your insides."

The *drip, drip, drip* of the church candles flashes. "But you asked about Katy, not my ex. I just thought it was important to give you context on how important my friends are to me."

His hand in hers is comforting. She goes on and makes full eye contact with him this time.

"So about Katy. Having to watch someone die over nine months is something I would never wish on anyone. She went in for a routine exam and they found skin cancer. They removed it, but the cancer was relentless in spreading. It made its way to her brain, and she wasn't the same after that. She was strong the entire time, putting on a brave face. She died less than a year after the diagnosis. That was last March. Her husband was understandably heartbroken, and she preferred for one of her girlfriends to take care of her at the end. I traveled back and forth to help. At the end, she couldn't talk, eat, or go to the bathroom. Someone needed to be the strong one, so I tried to support Katy, her husband, and the rest of my girlfriends through it.

"What I realize is that I have never really dealt with my own emotions about it. So the last couple of months I've kind of kept to myself and not done much with my friends. Instead, I've thrown myself into work, which I know isn't good either. The goal of the trip was to heal from all this. Then I met you, making it hard to focus on that. It's hard to heal when I have all of these feelings about…" Amy stops. She isn't ready to admit to herself, much less him, how much she likes him.

"About what?" he prompts her to finish.

"It's just, I like you, but I think being together is unrealistic. We both have careers; we live far apart. Maybe we should just let it be." A forced smile flashes on her face thinking about the song they'd heard earlier.

"Listen, I know we haven't known each other that long. But I want to know you better. I like you. With my travel schedule, it won't be easy, but we can figure it out."

His eyes beg her. "We'll see," she responds and

puts her other hand on top of his. "It's late, are you ready for sleep?"

"Sure. I have a flight to catch tomorrow." They both drop their heads on the pillows, and he reaches for her. As his shallow breathing deepens, she questions if maybe it was worth trying to make it work. She falls asleep, dreaming she's in a strange place and looking for Parker. She can't find him anywhere.

Chapter Thirteen
The Goodbye

The next morning, he pulls her close to him in bed.

"I know we kind of talked about it last night, but I'd like to see you again soon." He doesn't meet her gaze.

"C'mon, Parker, let's be realistic. We live states apart, you travel all the time for work, and I'm busy with my career. I think we should just let it be what it is and take it from there. Does that sound like a plan?"

"But what if I end up working in Washington?"

"Then we can totally hang out." She smiles. "What time is your flight?"

"It's at two. Do you want room service?"

She checks the clock on the bedside table. It's already eleven. *Makes sense that we slept so late. We didn't go to sleep until fucking four.* She processes the feelings they shared last night about love, life, divorce, and death.

"I always want room service."

Parker picks up the phone to call and orders bacon, scrambled eggs, and a Belgian waffle with strawberries and whipped cream. "Oh, and coffee. With cream."

I knew I liked this guy.

While they wait for the food, they cuddle naked on the bed.

They eat on his balcony. The sun is hot, and Amy

can't find one cloud in the sky. She smokes on the balcony while he packs. "I better head to the airport." His gaze shifts from hers, but not before she catches a glimpse of wetness in his eyes. Tears.

Amy smiles. "I'll walk you out."

Before he closes the door, she looks one last time at the rumpled sheets, rose petals, and the dried wax on the floor. She beams as the door clicks shut.

"Can I at least have your number?" He shifts his bags so he can grab her hand.

The lobby somehow looks different with her hand in his.

"Sure."

He sets down his bags, hands her his phone, and waves for a taxi.

Amy puts in her number and hesitates. A new possible relationship—and losing control—scares her to death after everything she's been through. She's hasty and swaps the last two digits, so it isn't her real number.

She hands him the phone. "Can I have yours?" She gives him her phone, and he puts his number in, labeling it as Parker with a heart next to it.

The taxi arrives, and he hugs her, brushes his lips on hers. "I'm really glad we met."

"I'll see you soon?" His eyes are hopeful.

"Yes, maybe." She doesn't want to see his sad eyes again.

She watches him get in the cab and drive away. Tears well in her eyes, and she wipes them, irritated.

She takes her phone out again and looks at his number and the heart he put next to his name.

Her hands shake as she deletes his number. It's

best to leave it as it was. Fun and uncomplicated. No emotions. No vulnerability. Maintain control.

She regrets her decision right away. It was so unlike her to be so impulsive. Maybe it was something more than a fling. She shakes her head to remove the thought. There are so many reasons why any future between them couldn't exist.

Chapter Fourteen
Regret

The long walk to her room is filled with regret. Deleting his number was a dumb move. *It's not like I had to text him or anything, but at least the option would still be there.* She flops onto the bed to try and shake the thoughts from her head. She tries to push away the bile building in her throat. *Fuck. Dumb.* Could she find him somehow, maybe through his company website? *Give it a day and see how you feel. Remember, this was supposed to be uncomplicated, and you need to work on you.* That hasn't changed. Or has it? The conversation with Parker about her ex-husband, indiscretions with Kevin, and the loss of Katy made her feel better and maybe even accept what's happened. Maybe even help her move on from it. Emma always says, "Everyone comes into your life for a reason, a season, or a lifetime." Maybe Parker entered her life for a reason. To help her see things in this new light. Perhaps she should just leave it at that. *He came into my life for a reason, and that's it.*

The room is made up because she didn't sleep there last night, and the beer can she used for an ashtray is gone too. She smiles when she glances at the couch where she rode Parker. It's lunchtime, but the huge breakfast still settles in her stomach. More coffee? *Nah, I'd be bouncing off the walls.* She shrugs and grabs a beer. *Five o'clock somewhere.*

She grabs her laptop, phone, beer, and cigarettes and sits on the balcony. The tropical sun beats down, making the chair warm on the backs of her thighs. *I should shower.* But the sweet smell of Parker is one she wants to hang onto. She shivers when she thinks of his hands all over her body, massaging her last night. Oh, and the candles. *What a romantic.* She texts Ava.

—*Hey sis. How's your day?*—

—*It's going good. Busy. How's your Bahamas lover?*—

—*He's good. We went out to a fancy dinner last night. I loved being on a "date."*—

—*So you're spending all your vacation time with him now.*—

—*Nope, he left this morning to go home.*—

—*Are you ok?*—

—*I'm fine. I liked him, we had fun, now it's over.*—

She isn't fine.

—*Do you think you'll see him again?*—

—*Nope. I deleted his number and gave him the wrong number.*—

—*Why'd you do that?*—

—*Because it wouldn't be anything more than it was. He lives far away, travels a lot for work, and I'm tied to the university. So what's the point in communicating with him if it'll go nowhere? Besides, I'm not looking for a boyfriend or husband. I just became free.*—

Despite the feigned confidence, her heart drops at the loss.

—*Very true. You'll find your prince charming, and maybe one that lives close.*—

—I don't think there's such thing as prince charming, nor am I sure I need one.—

If there is such thing as prince charming, it is probably Parker. She's nauseated over her impulsiveness in deleting his number. She reminds herself sometimes people just walk into your life unexpected and leave just as fast. And that's ok. Maybe they entered your life to teach you something. This still doesn't make her feel better.

—Disagree. Either way you've just gotten free from that horrible marriage. You should enjoy yourself for a while without being tied down. What are you going to do today?—

—I don't know yet, I may do a tour or something. Not sure if I want to sit by the pool. Tonight, I'm going to a nightclub with two girls I met a few days ago.—

—You meet people wherever you go.—

—Right?—

—Gotta get back to work. Have a perfect day.—

—You too. I love you.—

—I love you too.—

She puts her phone down and grabs her laptop. *What should I do today?*

I can't sit here and mope all day, I need a distraction. Amy googles, "Things to do in Nassau."

The top ten activities appear in an article. Graycliff and rum tour. Check. Atlantis Casino. Check. Horseback riding. No, thank you. Harbor tour. Sounds boring, no. Scuba diving shark adventure. Hmm, maybe? She clicks on the description of the activity. It describes the first dive as swimming in Stuart Cove's Dive Bahamas to see the wildlife. Then for the second dive, the divers sit on the bottom while a feeder entices

135

the sharks to come. *Humans should never feed sharks. Why do humans always have to fuck things up?* As much as she'd like to see sharks only a few feet away, she doesn't want to do it that way.

She clicks back to look at other options. Shopping. *No, thank you. Not a fan, unless on Amazon.* Amy thinks of her full Amazon cart, just waiting for her to press "place your order." A dive at Saddleback Cay. *Hmm.* She clicks on it. The cay is one of the outer islands in the Bahamas, and the beaches and water look stunning. She checks the times, and there's a tour company offering a half-day trip and dive there starting at one. She checks the time on her laptop. Perfect; it's twelve fifteen. She calls them and gives them her credit card number, and they say they will pick her up at the hotel at twelve forty-five. Amy rushes to put on her swimsuit and gather necessities, like sunscreen. She's ready in just a few minutes and grabs her phone to check Facebook before going downstairs. *I fucking love/hate Facebook.* On her feed, a memory comes up. Although the memory doesn't say this, it's the day Katy got her stage four cancer diagnosis. Katy's husband took the picture. They're sitting at a bar together, smiling and toasting the camera. Their eyes are puffy from crying. When their tears had dried, Katy caught her gaze sheepishly and had said, "Might as well go out and have a few drinks." Neither knew that was the beginning of the end, and Katy only had less than a year. She shakes her head and throws the phone in her bag, then heads downstairs.

While she's waiting, she sees the couple that was fighting in the pool two days ago. The woman is carrying their bag, and they're talking in low whispers when they stand near Amy. She tries to listen to what they're saying, *don't be fucking nosy*, but can't quite hear. There are quite a few other people standing in the lobby, also waiting for their tours. Excited chatter fills her ears as everyone watches the curb for their respective bus.

Her bus has "Diving Unlimited" painted in scrawling letters on the side. When she moves toward the curb to board, the fighting couple stands behind her. *Great. They're on the same dive trip, so I get to listen to them fucking fight all day.* She weaves her way down the aisle, the bus smelling like saltwater and sweaty wet suits.

A few people are already on the bus. The dive master, who's doubling as a tour guide, points out the sights to them and explains they will arrive at the marina, board the boat, then take off to Saddleback Cay. She introduces herself as Maria, and she's no older than twenty-one, cute and perky.

When they arrive at the bustling marina, Amy squeezes past other people on the dock boarding different tour boats. The long sandy beach next to the marina stretches out beside the aqua-blue water. *I think I could walk to my hotel from here.* A twinge of nausea fills her tummy when she sees the huge hotel casino she and Parker were at last night. The fighting couple linger behind on the dock, whispering in indistinct voices. Maria directs them to find a spot to sit that has the gear they'll need—a regulator, tanks, fins, a weight belt to help them sink, and a mask.

As everyone else gets settled and the boat takes off, Maria raises her voice to be heard over the excited chatter and engine. "Who would like to rent a wet suit?"

Yuck, Amy thinks. Even though it's tempting to be warm, they're nasty. No, thank you.

The fighting couple takes a seat right across from her. *Damn it.* The woman makes eye contact and introduces them both. "Hi, I'm Charla, and this is Michael."

She shakes her hand. "Hi, I'm Amy." Charla asks her where she's from, which begins small talk Amy doesn't want to engage in because it's distracting her thoughts away from Parker. She smiles and answers all of Charla's questions but doesn't ask any in return.

Maria talks about the dive, explaining it will be from the beach. The last time Amy did a beach dive, it was with her ex-husband in Maui. They had both certified a few days prior and went without a dive master. She had dragged the heavy equipment all the way to the beach from the parking lot. She forgot to secure the sand-filled beanbag shaped weights, so they fell out while they were swimming to the dive point. When it was time to sink, since the weights had disappeared, she wasn't able to float down to the bottom. She tried all the techniques she had learned to sink, but nothing worked. Her ex-husband, ten feet down, screamed at her silently through slanted eyes, angry bubbles of water exhaling from his regulator. He eventually surfaced and spoke between gritted teeth. "What the fuck is going on?"

"I think my weights fell out of my belt."

He came over to look. "They sure did because you didn't secure the Velcro. That is so stupid."

"I know. I'm sorry."

"You're sorry? That doesn't do us much good now,

does it? You need to be more careful. You are probably the only person in the world to lose weights. I'll try to pull you down."

Amy put the regulator in her mouth, and he jerked at her ankles to pull her down. She stayed at the surface.

He came up and growled, "If you'd lose a few pounds, you wouldn't have so much buoyancy and wouldn't need the weights at all, like me."

She bobbed in the water, not sure what to say. *I fucking hate you.*

"It's your fault we don't get to do this dive, and we'll have to pay for the weights. They sure as hell aren't coming out of our account. You can use your allowance to pay for them."

Amy felt stupid as she followed him to the shore. She was sure that she'd hear about this the rest of the trip. The surprising thing about that encounter was they were just a year into their marriage. She had it in her mind that things weren't bad until several years in. He had started out with small and infrequent comments that happened more often as time went on.

Hmmm. Why am I just now fucking remembering this? His control created a need for her to have more control over other things in her life. A bump in the water brings her to the present, and she shakes her head at the memory, staring at the vastness of the ocean.

In the distance, she can see Saddleback Cay. The water changes from aqua to dark blue one hundred feet from the shore. There are black spots under the water, indicating coral reefs. Her heart flutters, excited at the thought of getting to explore them up close. What would it be like to explore them with Parker? Maybe they'd frolic in the water together, swimming after each other and laughing through their regulators. He'd pull her close under the water, and they'd interlock hands. If only. She shakes the thought from her head. *That will never happen. He's gone. I fucked up.*

When the boat skims the water to land on the beach, Maria instructs all of them to take their equipment with them. The tanks are heavy; this is her least favorite part of diving.

The seven of them, plus Maria, drag the equipment onto the beach, the blistering heat beating down on them. A pool of sweat gathers in her swimsuit top. Maria outlines the route of the dive on a small whiteboard attached to her equipment. Without looking up, she says to Amy, "You'll be my dive buddy."

Everyone puts on their equipment, and there are sighs all around from the struggle of getting it on all while balancing on the searing sand in the heat. Michael and Charla get theirs on much quicker than Amy. She notices that while Charla struggles to pull the tank over her shoulders, Michael just watches her with a look of disgust on his face. Once Charla gets it on, she puts the regulator in her mouth to test it, and no air whistles through the regulator.

"Oh my God. How many times do I have to tell you? You gotta turn the air on before you put the tank and BCD on."

"Oh, shit. Can you turn it on for me?"

"Fuck no. You have to learn some time." He watches her struggle to take off the heavy BCD and tank, turn on the air, and put the heavy equipment back on. Her face is damp with sweat.

Amy curses him in her head.

Maria instructs them to get into the water. The cool water is a welcome relief; and a collective sigh emanates from the divers. They sink to the sandy bottom, then swim out toward the coral reefs.

Any sadness about Parker leaving and the anniversary of Katy's diagnosis float away. There's just the mechanical breathing, in and out, in and out.

The fake air in the tank clears her lungs and her mind of the negative thoughts that have followed her these last several months. The dive is calming, and the colorful coral dance underwater. Maria points out a nurse shark, and there are schools of fish cutting their eyes at her as they swim away. Amy reaches out to touch them, and they swim faster, bringing a flutter of delight to her stomach.

When it's time to surface, she paddles to the surface and notices that Charla is already up, but Michael isn't yet.

Maria pops up at the same time as Amy, her eyes wild, and takes the regulator out of her mouth and asks Charla, "What were you doing here?"

"I don't know. I just popped up." Charla clears her throat. Compressed air in the tank makes a diver's throat dry.

"Did you let air out of your BCD as we got shallower?"

"Shit, I forgot about that part."

"Are you okay?" Maria is no doubt worried about decompression sickness, which happens when people rise to the surface too fast.

"Yes, I feel fine. Thank you for asking." Amy floats in the water, the sun drying her face, head turned so she doesn't have to listen to what she's pretty sure comes next.

Michael thrashes to the surface, causing a splash. "What the fuck happened to you? You fucked up my dive because I couldn't see you anymore."

Charla challenges him, "As my dive buddy, shouldn't you have tried to come find me instead of being worried about your own dive? What if something bad had happened to me?"

"It's not my fault you're a shitty scuba diver. Fuck."

Amy's heart beats faster and her hands shake. She takes off her mask to wipe the salty tears welling in her eyes.

The rest of the afternoon, she avoids the two of them, not wanting to hear any more of him being an asshole. Maria puts an array of fresh fruit and cheese out for a snack, and Amy takes some to nibble on as she walks on the beach, alone, looking for shells.

The way Parker looked at her last night as he was about to come and how strong his hands were on her body were the only thoughts in her head. *I'm pretty sure it was really dumb to delete his number.* She shrugs. Too late to do anything about it now. *Just stop thinking of him.*

For the rest of the dive trip, she's unsettled. Everywhere she goes, Charla seems to find her and want to chat. Amy understands Charla's motivation, as she used to do the same thing. When your husband is an asshole, any chance you have to talk to someone else is a welcome distraction. She tries to be kind to her. When Michael goes to the bathroom, her insides churn and cause her to sit next to Charla. She whispers, "Listen, I don't know you, and it's not my place to say, but your husband is an asshole to you. Get out before fifteen years goes by, poof, leaving you to figure out where you went wrong. Stop wasting time."

Charla blinks, stares, and begins to respond when Michael comes back, grumbling under his breath.

Charla mouths, *Thank you.* Satisfied that maybe she made a difference, Amy shares a shy smile with Charla, just as they are told to board the boat for the journey back.

The water is rough on the way, and she can't hear Charla and Michael arguing above the roar of the engine and the waves slapping against the boat. *I hope she fucking takes my advice.* Peacefulness envelops her.

Chapter Fifteen
Nightclubs and New Girlfriends

Amy arrives in her room and tries to shake off the unsettled feelings. It's six p.m., and she texts Lynn and Jennifer to see what time they want to meet.

—*Hey. Hope you're having a great day. Still up for the club tonight?*—

—*Absolutely. Do you want to meet us at our hotel for a pre-going-out drink?*—

—*Sure, what time?*—

—*How about 9 at our hotel, in the lobby bar?*—

—*Great. BTW, what are you two wearing?*—

—*The sluttiest outfits we brought, LOL short dresses and heels.*—

—*Perfect. See you at 9.*—

She wanders to her closet to choose an outfit. She didn't bring any "club" wear and wonders if she's too old to go to a club. *Fuck it.* She tries to focus on what to wear instead. She chooses the strapless dress she wore last night. It smells like sex, Parker's pine-scented cologne, and sweat. She lays it out on the bed and chooses flats since her feet are blistered from last the heels last night.

She orders room service for dinner and sits on the balcony having a pre-drink of her own, smoking too many cigarettes. *I need to be fucking tipsy to go to any club.* She doesn't remember the last time she went to a club and is sure they don't play eighties hair band music. Oh well, it's better than moping here in the room.

Not really looking at the screen, she scrolls through *Facebook* on her iPad, and a new friend request catches her eye. She clicks on it, expecting it to be Lynn or Jennifer.

Oh my God, it's Parker. How did he find me?

Her stomach flips. Tingles rise from her feet to her head to her toes. *I never told him my last name.* She slaps her forehead, remembering she told him where she teaches, so finding her last name wasn't hard if he did a Google search. She stands on the balcony and does a little dance, her smile widening as the reality sets in. He isn't lost forever.

Amy accepts the request stat, so she doesn't lose him again. In one swoop, she clicks on his profile to read more about him. He posted a picture earlier today from the airport, with the word *homebound* on it. He's all smiles in the photo. She scrolls through and sees most of what he posts is funny memes. Hungry for more information, she continues to scroll through his page. His daughter has freckles, pigtails, and smiles wide in every picture. And just like he said, he travels a lot for work. She doesn't see pictures of other women, which was, admittedly, what she was looking for. At least he isn't a liar like Alejandro. Her heart jumps in her stomach when she sees a new message on the social media site from him. She opens it.

"So I tried to call you. It was the wrong number. I hope it's okay I found you here?" He puts a smiley face after it.

"Oh, it was? Shoot." She cringes as she types,

knowing she gave him the wrong number on purpose. Her heart skips a beat, and her body tingles at the effort he put in to find her. She writes, "I'm glad you found me here, too." She gives him her real phone number so she doesn't lose him again. *Fuck it.*

"How are you?"

"I'm doing good." She adds a smiley face.

"Amy, I miss you. I was looking at plane tickets to come see you in Washington. Would you like that?"

"Yes, I'd like that a lot. I can't stop thinking about you."

She surprises herself because it isn't a lie, yet her face flushes at the bluntness of her comment despite everything she'd promised herself about not being vulnerable with him.

"I've been thinking about you all day too. What'd you do today?"

She goes along with the subject change.

"Went scuba diving. It was awesome. Getting ready to go out with the two girls I told you I met."

"Oh, three gorgeous women about town. The guys had better watch out. I hope you have fun. I'll let you go for now. Chat later?"

"Yes. Bye for now." She likes that, although he hasn't met the two other girls, he assumes they are beautiful. Such a gentleman.

She prepares herself for disappointment. *Okay, I can admit that I really like him, but the fact remains he lives so far away.* This will be nothing more than what it was. There's that negativity again. Negativity, or reality?

She shakes away those thoughts, shuts her iPad, and jumps in the shower. She closes her eyes and reaches down to wash Parker off her pussy. The hot water runs over her breasts, and she shoves a finger inside, rubs her clit, and moans a solitary, needy, and impatient release.

After dinner, she changes into her chosen outfit and puts on light makeup. *I'll sweat it all off anyway.* She looks at herself in the mirror. She turns around in a circle to check herself out at every angle. *I'm okay. Maybe even sexy.* Then she grabs the little purse Parker got her and heads downstairs to catch a taxi to Lynn and Jennifer's hotel.

Jennifer and Lynn are waiting for her in the lobby bar. They both look super fucking hot. They curled their hair, and their skintight tops and skirts show off their perfect size-four figures. She wonders, for a second, if she's the fat friend tagging along—even though she's only a size ten. She scoffs at that idea. *I'm fine the way I am.*

"You look gorgeous." Jennifer stands to hug Amy.

"I didn't bring any club wear." She looks down at her outfit.

"I like the way you did your hair, and you are glowing," Lynn compliments.

Amy reaches to touch her barrette, holding her hair half up. The time she took to flat iron her bangs was useless. She brushes them out of her face and feels that the humidity has taken its toll on them. Orgasms will make you look better than you actually do any day of the week.

"Rum shots?" A devilish grin spreads across Lynn's face, referring to the other day.

"Fuck yes." She's already a little buzzed from drinking the beers in her room.

The women tell Amy about their last few days, then inquire about hers. "So have you been seeing that guy at your hotel?" Jennifer inquires.

"I have, but he went home today. I gave him the wrong number, but then he found me on *Facebook* and messaged me earlier."

"You're probably glowing because of all the sexy time you two had. And I get giving him the wrong number. No complications, right?" Jennifer and Lynn both giggle.

She agrees and laughs with them, although inside, she shakes her head with disagreement.

She tells them about her day scuba diving. "The dive was excellent, but that couple was so weird. I think I was out of line with what I told her."

"Men are assholes," Lynn says. "But I don't know, maybe you helped encourage her to do something she knows she already needs to do."

Jennifer agrees. Amy remembers things aren't going well between her and her husband. Maybe Jennifer needs to hear that too.

"Well, not all men are assholes," Amy responds, thinking of Parker, the rose petals, and the gentle way he grabbed her arm when she was struggling in heels.

"True, but they were taught to protect and provide. They're all kinds of confused now that we women are so independent."

There may be something to that. Although her ex-husband was always somewhat mean, he was meaner after she earned her master's degree. She tucks that thought into her mind for later consideration.

"Oooh, look." Lynn points out two attractive men walking into the lobby soaking wet—fresh from the pool. They're tan, and the water from their bodies leaves a trail on the floor.

"Oooh." Jennifer pretends to wipe drool from her lip. "I'd like to be sandwiched in between those two."

She agrees, although all she can think about is the heat Parker's body created next to hers.

The three of them have a few more drinks and are ready to take a taxi to the club at eleven p.m. *At home, I'd have been in bed for two hours already.*

As they wait in line at the nightclub, Amy fingers her hair, afraid they won't let her in as happens at some clubs for those who aren't "good enough." She tries not to think of the resulting embarrassment if they tell her she isn't allowed because she's too old, too—or not enough—something else. When they get to the front, the bouncer just waves them through after checking their IDs. She breathes a sigh of relief.

When she follows the two women into the club, the heavy beat of bass thumps in her chest. Jennifer turns around to say something to Amy, but it's impossible to hear. Instead, Jennifer just uses gestures to indicate that they get a drink at the bar. Amy nods.

She squeezes through the hot, sweaty bodies to make it to the bar. Jennifer and Lynn swagger more confidently in their heels than she did last night. The cigarette smoke rises to the vaulted ceiling, and the DJ plays above the dance floor. The purple lights make his face shine eerily. She wipes other people's sweat from her arms, a bit disgusted. Jennifer and Lynn are already taking a shot when she makes it to the bar. They hand her one. The clear alcohol hits her bloodstream right away, makes her head spin, and she loosens up, swaying to the music.

The explosive drumbeats roar in her ear, making it difficult to focus. She can't make the words out, only the bass beat that resonates throughout her body. *Excellent fucking place to people watch.* She takes in the atmosphere and sees couples "dirty dancing" and tries to think of the more contemporary term for it. Oh, right, grinding? Or is it freak dancing?

Everyone, wearing impeccable outfits, is flirting and laughing. How can they hear each other? Jennifer tries to say something to her, but she just points to her ears. Lynn and Jennifer talk to a guy at the bar, and Lynn pulls on Amy's arm so she joins the conversation. He's young and very good looking, his blue eyes appearing bluer set against his dark skin. She just nods and smiles when it seems appropriate to do so.

It's sweltering, so Amy decides to step outside. She grabs Lynn's arm and lifts her fingers to her mouth like she's smoking a cigarette, and points to the door. Lynn understands and nods, turning her gaze to the hot guy. Afraid if she goes out the front, they won't let her back in, she wanders around until she finds a bouncer at what appears to be a back door. It's quieter here.

"Is this to the outside?" She questions the dark-skinned bouncer.

"Yes, but you can't go out there."

"Please? I'm so hot, and I just need some air and a cigarette."

He nods, accepting the ten-dollar bill she thrusts into his hand. "Knock when you're ready to come in," he instructs her.

Amy takes a deep breath as she steps into the alley. The huge dumpster there stinks like garbage and vomit, but at least it's not so loud. People are yelling on the streets, but it's muffled. She lights a cigarette. The smoke fills her lungs, and she sighs, pushing her sweaty bangs out of her eyes.

The same bouncer opens the door for her when she's done. Relieved to have a bit of quiet, she steps in and again makes her way past the clammy people to the bar to find the women. Maybe it's the drinks, but the noise bothers her less this time. She finds Jennifer and Lynn, and they're no longer talking with the man. Instead, one is grinding on him from behind, the other from the front. They see her and motion for her to come join them. She shakes her head and points to the bar and cups her hand like she's holding a glass.

Her heart pounds to the rhythm of the music.

Amy squeezes in at the bar and waves around a twenty-dollar bill. The bartender's gaze meets hers, and he raises an eyebrow instead of asking what she wants. He skips the other people who'd been waiting. She gives them a sideways glance, shrugs her shoulders, and orders a beer, despite her guilt. When it comes, she turns around to people watch and leans on the sticky bar.

A man in his late twenties comes to her, smiles, and says something in her ear. She can't hear.

"What?" Amy shouts at him, pointing to her ear.

"Looks like you're having a good time." She reads his lips.

"Yep." She grins at him. He's cute, the white T-shirt hugging his muscular chest.

"Wanna dance?"

She nods and takes a large swallow of beer so it doesn't spill while she's dancing.

Other people's bodies and thrashing hips crash into

her as she moves. Annoying. *This is why I don't go to clubs anymore.* Too many damn people. She glances at Jennifer and Lynn. Another man has joined their dancing threesome, making it a foursome. Amy can't help but admire the effortless way their hips and arms move to the music as they dance.

The cute white T-shirt guy grabs her by the waist and turns her around, so her ass is facing him. He moves his hips in large circles, bouncing his package against her. She can feel his ampleness through his black jeans with every brush his crotch makes on her ass.

Her thoughts wander to Parker. *We didn't get a chance to dance together. I wonder if we ever will.* She thinks about the places she will take him if he really comes to Washington to visit. One of them will have to be a place where they can dance.

Holding a hand over her mouth to conceal a yawn, she turns around and lifts a finger to the guy to show she'll be right back. She finds her private door again.

The same bouncer is working. "Need a break?" He chuckles.

"You know it."

He pushes open the door for her to smoke as she did before. She doesn't give him money this time, and he doesn't appear to expect it.

Her ears continue to ring despite the silence. There's a beep from her phone, and she clicks on the notification for the *Facebook* message. It's Parker. Her stomach does a flip-flop. The loneliness that crept inside her in the club and on the island disappears.

Shifting her cigarette into her other hand, she swipes to read his message.

—Miss me yet?—

—Yes.—

She adds a smiley face.

—It's so loud in here. I think I may be too old for clubs.—

—You're only as old as you feel.—

He sends a selfie of him and his daughter.

—Awwww so cute. Are you having dinner together?—

—Yes, at her favorite place, Roadside Grill.—

—That's awesome.—

—I looked at plane tickets to Washington earlier and I want to run some dates by you. Can we FaceTime tomorrow?—

—Yes, that sounds great.—

Her heart flutters, and the corners of her mouth turn into a grin. *So I guess he really is serious about coming to see me.*

—Ok, please be safe. Talk soon.—

—Yes, talk soon.—

Her heart aches. She inhales the last drag of her cigarette. Just as she turns toward the door, it opens, and she has to step back to avoid being hit by it.

It's the white T-shirt guy.

"How'd you find me?" Amy raises her eyebrows.

"I followed you, then had to tip the bouncer to let me out here with you." *I guess the bouncer is loyal to no one except the Bahamian dollar.*

She glances around at the darkness and emptiness of the alley. Her heart beats quicker.

He asks her name and says his is Michael. Ugh. Like the guy from earlier. He explains he's a local and moved down from Miami a few years ago. He bums a cigarette from her and asks about her trip so far. They make small talk, *ugh*, about the beaches and Saddleback Cay. He's boring as fuck. There doesn't appear to be much going on with him except how cute he looks in the T-shirt.

"I'm going to head inside." She hugs herself and fakes a shiver.

"I want to kiss you. Can I?" he asks her.

Her head spins, and the smell of the alley churns her stomach.

"Sure." She isn't sure why she answers yes, except the fact she doesn't need to have loyalty to anyone right now as she isn't in a relationship with anyone. One kiss can't hurt, right? It might feel good. Numb the feelings for Parker. *Parker could be bullshitting about coming to Washington and missing me and all that.*

He takes her chin in his hand and brushes his lips against hers, and she can taste the whiskey on his breath. He thrusts his tongue into her mouth like a snake, in, out, in, out. She tries to slow him down by pulling away from his chest, then moves to kiss his neck so as not to be attacked by his tongue. It's disgusting.

He gives her ass a hard squeeze.

Amy yearns for it to be Parker.

He reaches his hand under her skirt. She pushes it away. He takes her hand and puts it on his throbbing bulge. She moves her hand away.

"Wanna suck my dick?"

God, this guy can't take a hint. "No."

"Seriously? But your kisses got me all hot."

"Yep." Amy pulls away and knocks on the door, praying the bouncer will answer.

The white T-shirt guy grabs her from behind by the wrists.

"Let go of me. I'm going back inside."

He releases her, and the bouncer opens the door and smiles at her. Her gaze narrows and she glares.

Well, fuck. There's a chance that may have taken a turn for the worse. Amy shakes it off and scours the club for Jennifer and Lynn. She finds them near the bar.

Her head is spinning, and she isn't sure if it's because of the white T-shirt guy encounter, the drinks, or the heat of the club.

She finds her friends near the bar. They smile when they see her.

Where were you? Jennifer mouths.

"Needed some air," Amy screams in her ear.

"We were worried about you, was coming to look for you. We're glad you're okay."

Amy's heart soars and is grateful these girls are looking out for her. It's like home, and the loneliness fades away again, but just a little.

I need to sit down for a second, Lynn mouths, and they move toward a back room, where they discover another bar, tables, and chairs. The quiet is a welcome reprieve.

They each order a beer and find a back table.

"I saw you talking to that super sexy white T-shirt guy. Are you going to take him to your room?" Jennifer smirks.

"Nah, he's kinda a jerk." She doesn't explain further. "I just got a message from Parker. He sent me a picture of him and his daughter."

"Honey, remember, it was just a vacation fling. But are you thinking about getting involved with him?"

Jennifer raises her right eyebrow at her.

"There's something about him I can't put my finger on. I like him. He said he wants to come out to Washington to see me. I want him to."

"What does it hurt to go for it? I mean, in regular life as opposed to vacation life, it could be different, but you won't know unless he comes out to see you. Stranger things have happened."

Jennifer and Lynn look at each other, and both of their eyes light up at the same time.

"Oh, like that acquaintance of ours. She'd travel from Oshkosh to El Paso for work all the time. She'd go to this place for dinner every night while traveling and ended up connecting well with the bartender. They had a casual relationship for, what, probably two years." Lynn looks to Jennifer for confirmation.

"Yes, it was about that long. Then he moved to Oshkosh, and they've been together ever since. They even have a baby now." Jennifer's gaze looks wistful.

"Really? Wow. I just don't want to be dumb about it, you know?" She looks at her half-drunk beer, and her stomach clinches as she waits for their response.

"Seriously, what do you have to lose?" Jennifer peers over her beer at her.

"Good point."

They drink a couple more beers and chitchat about their lives in their respective hometowns. The easy conversation, seamlessly moving from topic to topic, is like being with her girlfriends. She misses them and swears to set up a girl's weekend as soon as she's home.

"Well." Jennifer gathers her bag. "What do you girls think? Are we ready to go?"

"I'm fine leaving if you're ready." Lynn gathers her purse, which has fallen on the sticky wooden floor.

"Let's do it." They stand and walk out of the club together. She peers at her phone, and it's already three a.m. *It seems like we just got here.*

The cab drops Amy off first, and the girls share backseat taxi hugs and promise to keep in touch. She can hear the cab idling until she's out of sight.

Something about the conversation with the women makes her walk lighter. Even though she didn't like the club itself much, she's glad she met them. *I'm pretty sure I'll see them again.*

She gets to her room, settles on her balcony with ice water, and messages Parker.

—I know it's late, so I don't expect you to respond, but just wanted to let you know I made it back to my room safe. I hope you had a great night with your daughter and I'm excited to talk with you about Washington trip plans.—

She sees three dots, showing he's texting. Her stomach flutters.

—It is late here, LOL, but I'm glad you messaged. After I dropped my daughter off, my best friend, Zach, stopped by. He's going through a hard time in his marriage, and we had a few drinks until he passed out on the couch. LOL. I'm heading to bed now, though. Can't wait to talk with you later about our plans.—

—Me either. Good night.—

—Good night. Dream of me.—

Oh, I'm sure I will. She settles into bed, not sure if she's drunk still or just drunk on the thought of seeing Parker when she thought she'd lost him forever.

Chapter Sixteen
Realizations

Waking up hungover is getting old. Amy slithers out of bed and heads to the bathroom, making a stop to order room-service coffee and a basket of sweet rolls. *That will make me feel better.* She swallows the bile climbing in her throat. When she tries to smoke, she dry heaves, puts out the cigarette, and lies in bed. When she hears the knock, she stands, and the blood flows to her head. She grabs the edge of the bed for support. As soon as the room-service person leaves, she pours coffee, savoring the first sip of coffee and real cream, and digs through the basket to find the roll she was hoping was there—the lemon cream-filled one. She takes a tiny bite at first, then picks at the edges where it's crispier. Better.

She sees her phone light up and grabs it while sipping coffee.

—*Hey how was your big night out?*—

—*Ugh. I feel like shit. I'm never mixing rum and beer again.*—

—*So it was a good night?*—

She doesn't tell Ava about the white T-shirt guy.

—*Yes, the two girls I met are awesome. I suspect our paths will cross again for sure.*—

—*I'm glad to hear that. I worried about you being lonely on the trip. What did you end up doing yesterday during the day?—*

—I went diving. It was fun except there was this couple there, and he was such an asshole to her. It was hard to watch.—

—How was he an ass?—

—He just kept putting her down even when she made a mistake that anyone could make.—

—That sounds familiar.—

—What do you mean?—

—Your ex was like that. It was hard to watch for all those years.—

—Yes. I got out. I should have gotten out sooner, but at least I did it.—

—How's Mom after the fall? BTW don't tell her I went diving, you know how she worries.—

—My lips are sealed. She's fine. Do you regret not giving your vacation lover your phone number today?—

—He found me on Facebook. We've messaged back and forth a few times. I think he may even come see me in Washington.—

—I thought you had decided you didn't need a price charming.—

—I still don't, but I genuinely liked him. It'll be fun to see where it goes. It may go nowhere, but I think I'm going to try.—

—Yeah, it could be fate although I know you're more of a believer of creating your own destiny. I kinda wish you'd explore a bit more rather than jumping into a relationship though.—

—I'm not jumping into anything. A visit doesn't mean we're getting married.—

—All I'm saying is just take things as they come.

You don't need to decide right now.—

    —You're right.—

She can almost see the toothy grin Ava displays when she's proud for saying or doing the right thing.

    —Gotta go. Meeting in five minutes. When do you fly home?—

    —I fly home tomorrow. I land in Seattle around 9 p.m. Then of course I have the long drive home over the mountain pass.—

    —Text me when you land, Sis. I love you.—

    —I love you, too.—

Ava's right. Amy will just take things as they come with Parker. No expectations. *If nothing else, it means I get to have great sex again.*

She takes her time drinking coffee and eats all the sweet breads in the basket. *Diet when I get home.* Even as she tells herself this, she knows she won't diet and is okay with this realization.

A beach day allows for a bit more sun and reading. The book doesn't make her as sad as it did before. It's better for Katy to be where she's at rather than suffering. *Damn, though, that doesn't mean I can't still miss her.*

Throughout the day, she alternates between swimming in the ocean and reading. The ocean is refreshing, like lemonade on a sultry summer day, and she smiles, looking at the spot where she and Parker made out in the water. She tries not to think about the cold, lifeless winter at home she'll go to tomorrow. Parker's impending visit makes the cold and dark seem less sad.

When the sun goes down, she shivers, so she heads upstairs, more at peace than she has been this entire trip and unsure why.

Amy left her phone in her room all day, not wanting to take his call next to others on the beach. She wanted to savor their conversation in private.

She checks, and he's called twice. She grins and her stomach flip-flops. She dials him using video.

Chapter Seventeen
A Beginning?

He answers right away.

"Hey, sexy." His wide grin causes a flutter in her heart. "You look like you just got back from the beach."

Amy looks at what she's wearing. She is still in her swimsuit cover-up, her messy bun is windblown, and her bangs are wild. *I didn't even think about freshening up before calling. Oh fucking well.*

"You got some good sun today, but not burned. Katy would be happy." He smiles.

She flushes at the fact he remembers her telling him about Katy and her illness, and her own subsequent addiction to sunscreen.

"Show me your tan lines."

She pulls down her cover-up and swimsuit top to show the tan line just above her nipples. He whistles. "I wish I could trace those tan lines with my fingers."

She sighs. "Me too."

"I've been meaning to ask you; can I have your address?"

Amy gives him the address, and they chitchat about their day and her night at the club. She leaves out the white T-shirt guy but tells him all about Jennifer and Lynn. She even tells him about the happy-sad feeling to see the best friends together and how it made her miss Katy but made her grateful for her other best girlfriends.

"I'm talking a lot. Tell me more about your friend Zach. I remember you mentioning him being a childhood friend, but you didn't mention he was having issues with his wife. What's up there?"

"Ugh, poor guy. His wife is not interested in having sex anymore. It started after they had a couple of miscarriages. They've decided not to have children now, but he's trying to figure out methods to woo her into the passion they had before. I've known her almost as long as I've known Zach. They've been together since we were fifteen. We used to double date."

"Double date?" She glances from her phone, pushing the jealousy down.

"Are you jealous?"

"No, of course not. We've both had pasts," she lies.

"Amy, I want to know everything about you, good, bad, and ugly. I want to know what you're like when you're stressed at work. I want to know about your family, what you love, and what you hate. For example, I don't even know what you look like in winter clothes."

She shrugs. Is this guy for fucking real?

She changes the subject. "Give me a tour of your house."

His eyes twinkle, and he jumps up, turning his phone around so she can see his living room. She remembers him mentioning at the casino dinner he'd bought the house in depths of sadness after his divorce and put all his energy into fixing it up. When he'd talked about that, he was proud of all the work he'd put in.

"Let's start outside."

He doesn't put on a jacket to protect himself from what looks to be frigid weather. *Ugh, I'll be going back to that kind of temperature tomorrow.*

The house is a blue craftsman style and looks way too big for one adult and a part-time daughter. He takes his phone inside and explains how he pulled up laminate floors to discover original wood floors from the 1920s house. He refinished them himself. The house is cute and decorated modern, mostly red, black, and yellow. There are throw pillows and rugs everywhere that pull the rooms together. He shows her his favorite room, the man cave, complete with a bar he made from whiskey barrels and a pool table. His speech quickens when he tells her about all the work he did.

A man who can do shit. That's sexy. Amy's ex-husband had no idea how to do any of that. She corrects herself. *You need to quit comparing.* This is something new, and he's a totally different man. Thank God.

He sits down on his black leather couch, and she asks him about the reunion with his daughter. Parker tells her how amazing it was to hug her. He goes on to explain his ex-wife has a new boyfriend who seems cool and a good stand-in stepdad for his daughter. *God, he's so mature.* She thinks of her friends who have divorced and how they just had nasty things to say about the new partner.

Amy takes a deep breath. "Your house is nice, but I'd like you on this couch right now." She turns the phone to the spot they fucked on the other night.

"Damn, I wish I were there too," he drawls. Has his Southern accent gotten stronger?

"Do you wanna have FaceTime sex?" There's a twinkle in his eyes.

"Yes, but first things first. You said you were looking at tickets to come out and see me?"

"Oh yes. I didn't want to pressure you." He grins. "So my Dubai install has been pushed back, so I don't need to leave for quite some time. How does next week for a visit sound?"

Her stomach alternates between giddy excitement and churning. It's so soon.

"I can be there the day after Christmas because I have my daughter on Christmas day. I can stay through New Year's. You're still on winter break during that time, right?"

She flashes him an enormous smile. "I can't wait to see you."

Amy forgets about any plans she had for keeping this relationship casual. Her brain is flashing *yes, yes, yes* like a neon sign.

"Great, I'll get the flight and text you the information. Now, where were we?" He holds his phone down so she can see him unbuttoning his jeans.

She shivers when his cock pops out of his pants.

"Tell me what you want me to do."

"I want you to rub your shaft, from top to bottom, slowly."

He obeys.

"Get some lotion, squirt it into your hand, and rub faster."

While he sets the phone down to get lotion, Amy takes off her cover-up and swimsuit and lies on the bed. She sets her backpack on the bed so she can set the phone up from below.

"Oh wow. I missed that view." He rubs lotion in his hands. "Tell me what you want to do to me." He tugs on his dick and sets the phone on pillows between his legs, then stretches across the couch, his head on the arm rest. The close-up of his throbbing dick makes her mouth water and sends an ache through her veins. She puts two fingers in her pussy, making slow circles with her fingers around the outside, then shoves one and two fingers in. She moans.

Through her moan, she demands, "I want you to stroke yourself hard and fast." He responds by gripping his dick tight and sliding his hand from the shaft to the tip.

She matches the rhythm of her fingers to his strokes and moans uncontrollably. "If you were here, I'd be riding your cock, sliding up and down hard and fast. Then I'd turn around and reverse cowgirl you so you could watch your cock slide in and out of me."

"Ohhhh." His head tips back. His strokes get faster, which she knows after being with him means he's nearing orgasm.

"I want you to come in me." She closes her eyes, imagining he's pounding his fingers inside of her. Not wanting to miss the show she knows is close, she opens her eyes again and begs, "Please come. I want you to come."

That's all it took. He moans, eyes closed, and the sight of his dick shooting cum all over his hands and the couch pushes her to the brink. Seeing his metamorphosis of pleasure from this view is thrilling. His body shudders.

He continues to stroke, increasing the intensity, letting out gasps of air. His cum-soaked hands and the close-up of his shooting cum make her pant.

She tips her head back, rubbing her clit from the

top to the bottom, only pausing to press her thumb to her clit, and like a flood, she squirts all over her hands and the bed. Her body shakes and shudders, and she gasps for breath. "Ohhhhh." She moans, needing a moment to make the blackness and red tracers in her eyes go away.

Parker is the first to speak. "Wow. I'd much rather been inside you, but I loved the view."

In between deep pants, she says, "Yes, me too."

They collect themselves and chat for a bit longer. When they hang up, she misses his smile, his laugh, and his voice. These feelings about him are unexpected.

After showering, she packs her bags to get them ready for her flight tomorrow. She opens her backpack to find the flight and hotel paperwork she shoved in there days before and checks her flight time. A lot has happened since then.

When she shoves the paperwork in, she notices the journal she brought and intended to write in everyday on her trip. She snorts to herself. *I guess I got a little distracted.*

Chapter Eighteen
One Last Night

Walking down the pathway one last time, her head is heavy and stomach twists. She doesn't want to leave.

She chooses a seat at the bar, and Jaden smiles wide when he sees her. "Beer?" He's already getting it before she answers yes. "What'd you do last night?"

"I went out with some girls I met a few days ago. It was a bust, though."

"Bummer. Where'd you go?"

She tells him the name of the nightclub, and he frowns.

"Ugh. Wish you'd told me. I would've warned against it. Everyone around here knows there are mostly local creepers preying on tourists at that club."

Her mind flashes to icky white T-shirt guy. "Yeah, I can see that. It was fun, though, to hang out with new friends. They remind me of my girlfriends at home. By the way, did your Tinder date ever get in touch with you?"

He smiles wide and leans on the bar. "She did. I took her out last night."

"Oh yeah?" The temptation to grab his hand and squeeze it like an old friend is too great, so she does. He squeezes her hand back.

"She takes care of her mom, who is sick, and her mom was having a terrible night."

"That seems like a good reason to cancel." He's so sweet; she's happy for him. "Judging by the look on your face, it was good?"

"Yeah, we had an incredible time. We plan to get together again tonight."

"That's awesome. What's her name?"

"Sydney." He wipes the bar with the rag and stares at the ocean, his gaze a million miles away.

For a few seconds, the only sound is the distant ocean waves lapping at the sand. "So as a bartender at a resort, you must see lots of crazy things. What is the craziest thing you've seen?"

"First, I am a bartender, but I'm also a writer. I'm almost finished with a political thriller that I hope to get published."

"I had no idea. That's awesome."

"Bartending pays the bills until I get rich and famous. But the craziest things I've encountered, hmm. Let me think about that."

A minute goes by, and they both stare at the ocean. In most situations, silence is awkward, but with Jaden, it isn't. He's like an older brother. The palm trees whisper in the breeze.

"Okay, here's one. It was about a year ago, and there was this attractive couple in their fifties on vacation. They were sitting at the bar, and when his wife went to the bathroom, he admitted to me he was having a hard time getting a hard-on. I remember thinking it was odd he told me this. They came to the bar every night during their two-week trip. Seven nights in, she was still in their room, and he came to the bar. He asked me if I'd be interested in being the bull in their cuckold relationship. I had to ask him what *bull* meant. He explained he'd like me to fuck his wife while he watched. He offered me a thousand dollars."

"Holy shit." Amy had heard of cuckolding before, but only in porn.

"I told him no. It was for no other reason than the fact I saw them fighting a lot of the trip and knew that would just make things worse."

"So was the guy mad you said no?"

"He wasn't. In fact, he tipped over five hundred dollars during their two-week trip. When I pointed out cuckolding wouldn't save their relationship, he agreed and appeared to be more in tune and flirty with his wife. On their last night, he confided to me he got it up, and they had amazing sex the night before."

"So you're a bartender, a writer, and also a saver of marriages?" She grins at him, and he grins back, the lights at the bar making his teeth shine red.

"Pretty much." He laughs.

She squirms in her seat, liking this comfortable, fun conversation. "Have you ever been married?"

"I was close once. There was a gorgeous local woman I dated for years, but she broke my heart."

"If you don't want to talk about it, it's okay, but how did she break your heart?"

"She cheated on me with my best friend. That was like fifteen years ago when I was thirty-five, so I kinda need to get over it." He chuckles, but his eyes are sad.

Amy's stomach is in knots, as she can't imagine the pain. "I'm so sorry."

"Yeah. I guess better to find out before I asked her to marry me, but still. I lost my best friend *and* my girlfriend."

"Are they still here on the island?"

"Nah, they both moved to the States, and last I heard, they have two kids together.

"That sucks."

"Yeah, but I'm over it, for the most part anyway. It's just hard to meet anyone on this island."

"I can see that. Not the same, but I live in a small town, and it's hard to meet people without everyone knowing your business."

Amy asks Jaden about his book. He talks fast, nearly out of breath. He becomes more animated than she's seen him. He enquires about her writing.

"It's mostly research stuff, kinda boring,"

"That's not boring. I don't know how people can do that."

He changes the subject and asks her about Parker. "Seems like you two were getting along pretty well."

"Yes, for sure. I *FaceTimed* with him earlier, and he's coming to visit me next week in Washington."

"Really? That's great. He's a respectable guy. We got to know each other pretty well since he was down here for so long. He's invited me to Nashville, and I'm hoping to go when he returns from Dubai."

The bar booms. Judging by the sound of the loud chatter and laughter, the patrons have been drinking all day by the pool. Jaden blasts the music, and the swoon of country music comes on. Her thoughts drift to Parker. Goose bumps appear on her arm at the thought of him coming to see her next week. She turns to stare at the ocean. Although it's dark, she imagines the waves crashing. The wind blows, and the breeze tickles her skin. *I will fucking miss this.*

Amy's phone beeps. It's Lexi, one of her oldest friends from high school. She's never been married, never intends to, and is somewhat impulsive and wild. Just two of Lexi's best qualities.

—Hey, girl. How's your trip?—

—It's great, but I'm headed home tomorrow.—

She sends a sad face.

—Hey, so this is random, but I just got an offer through work to go to Egypt in March. It's super cheap and it might be during your spring break. Do you want to go with me?—

Amy doesn't hesitate. Once, she traveled to the Peruvian Amazon and got to swim with pink dolphins. The Nile River has them, too. Egypt has been on her bucket list ever since.

—Fuck yes.—

—Cool. I'll put the package on hold, and we can work out details when you're home. We have three days to book after it's been on hold.—

Her heart flutters. Travel excites her like nothing else, except maybe Parker.

—Perfect. Love you.—

—Love you too. Safe travels.—

Just as she puts her phone down, she receives a group text from Lexi. Lexi also sent it to her sister and her two best friends—Natalie and Emma.

—Hey, girls. Thinking about planning another girl's weekend. Vegas? We can stay at my mom's time-share.—

—I'm down.— Natalie texted.

—100% in.— Emma added.

—Yes, just need to see if I can get someone to watch the kids.— Ava said.

—Cool. Let's talk more about it when we get together for the girl's gift exchange party this

weekend.— Lexie added a smiley face.

Shit. I forgot about that. Well good. I'll be able to tell *them about Parker at the same time. Hopefully, my sister hasn't already spilled the beans.*

Natalie sends a meme that shows a group of girls drinking out of enormous wine glasses. Amy chuckles.

"And what are you laughing at?" Jaden wipes down the bar in front of her and exchanges her ashtray.

"I just have the best girlfriends." She turns the phone to show him.

He grins.

She puts her phone down and chats more with Jaden, and for the most part, about Parker.

"I'm thrilled for you. I think that's so cool."

When she's ready to leave, he comes around the bar and hugs her.

"Good luck with Sydney."

"Good luck with Parker."

He's still waving at her as she walks around the corner, down the pathway, for the last time.

Chapter Nineteen
Homebound

Amy flies out of bed the next morning. It's already ten thirty a.m. *Travel days suck.*

When she arrives at the airport, there's no line at security, thank God. Security is easy and, with an hour to spare, sits in one of the ugly plastic chairs. She buys water from a vending machine and pops an anxiety pill. *First one since I've been down here.* Airports and being on an airplane are two of her least favorite things in life. Too bad travel is one of her favorite things.

She texts Parker.

—*Hey, how are you? What are you up to?*—

—*I'm doing good, thinking about you. I can't wait until we're together again. Just a little over a week away.*— He adds a smiley face at the end.

—*Yes. I can't wait.*—

—*You headed home?*—

—*Yep. At the airport. What are you up to today?*—

—*I'm having lunch and a few beers with friends, waiting for them at the bar now.*

—*Cool, I'll let you go then.*—

—*Okay. Let me know when you make it home safe.*—

—*I will.*—

—*Bye for now, sweetheart.*—

Sweetheart. Her heart melts.

She checks *Facebook*. She sees two new friend requests from Lynn and Jennifer. She accepts them and scrolls through the women's profiles. Amy sees they have tagged her in a photo the three of them took while at the nightclub and accepts the tag. Then she sends them a message.

—Hey, ladies, it was great to meet you. We should totally plan a girl's trip soon.—

Three dots shows she's responding.

—Yes. Let's stay in touch. Sometime this summer?—

—Absolutely.—

Maybe she'll invite Lynn and Jennifer to Las Vegas with her other girlfriends? She smiles. She has always loved meeting new friends. Unlike what often happens when you meet new people and never end up staying in touch, she suspects these two women will become true friends over the long haul. Friends for a lifetime, not for a reason or a season.

She shoves her phone in her bag and sees the hardback journal she brought again. She fishes a pen from her bag and begins writing.

December 20, the Bahamas

I was supposed to write in this journal every day while on my travels. I neglected to do it, like I sometimes do with everything but work. I wanted to capture the vibe and feeling of the place I was visiting. I am in the Nassau, Bahamas, and airport after a week sitting in the sun, scuba diving, rum tasting, and nightclubbing.

My intention for the trip was to focus on relaxing and work through some of the shit that's happened over the last year. Turns out being distracted helped the events of the last year come into clearer focus. I don't know if there is any way to "work through" some of these issues. Perhaps you learn to live with them and chalk it as learning.

On this trip, I thought a lot about my failures and fear of failure. How I cheated, how I was with a married man, how failure would happen if I didn't work every day. What if I were to think more about my successes instead of past or potential future failures? How do I do this? How does anyone do it when they rise from the ashes? Yes, I know that's super corny, but it feels true. They just plug away and do what feels right in the moment. Just like I've done on this trip.

The attendant calls Amy's boarding group from the microphone, and it crackles, so she only hears half of it. It distracts her from writing. She follows the herd to board the plane, then squishes into 22F, a window seat. She continues writing as the whir of the engines start.

On this trip, I thought a lot about Katy and the pain of missing her. I don't know what to do about this. It doesn't feel like it will fade away soon. My heart drops in my stomach when I think about losing her. The realization I've come to is the fact she isn't suffering anymore, and that's enough to dull the pain a bit.

I hate to say it, but the highlight of my trip wasn't the palm trees or the ocean. It was meeting a man I think I may have a deep connection with. Not only was the sex amazing, but already, I feel like I can talk with him about anything. I'm always trying to be in control of everything, I needed a vacation to, well, just allow those emotions. Instead of overthinking. I told him about Katy and remembered that talking about it is healing in itself.

New experiences can help you forget the old, negative ones. Well, maybe not forget, but at least be able to accept them. Maybe healing happens by being open to new things and accepting the old ones, for better or for worse.

Feeling satisfied the journal entry tied all of her thoughts together, she puts the notebook away, hitting her neighbor to the left with her arm, and mumbles, "Sorry." She sleeps the rest of the way.

When Amy lands in Seattle, she dreads the three-hour drive home. She takes the shuttle bus to her car and scrapes the ice off. She shivers, already missing the warm weather. Eighties hair band music keeps her entertained on the freeway, abandoned because of the late hour.

There are red roses on her doorstep when she arrives home. She smiles and opens the card. It reads, *Beautiful roses for a beautiful woman. To many more rose-filled beds in our future. Hugs and Kisses, Parker.*

The vase is cold from the air temperature, and she's careful to place her hands around the glass, so she doesn't drop it. She sets them on the dining room table, pausing to look at them. She sets the card next to the flowers and smiles. *To many rose-filled beds in our future.* This is moving fast. *And I don't care.* It feels right.

She cranks the heat, sways around the living room to the lyrics stuck in her head from the song she heard with Parker the other night, something about everything working out.

She takes off her jewelry and fingers the bracelet she always wears except on vacation for fear of losing it. She rubs her fingers across the engraving that says,

"Best friends forever." It was a gift from Katy after she got sick. Instead of being sad, she smiles. She was lucky to have known someone like Katy. Now she focuses on her other friends, being present, savoring each moment with them.

She scavenges for cheese and crackers, fixes a plate of goodies, and puts it on the couch. For the first time, she realizes she isn't eating at the kitchen table, like her ex always insisted. She drops a cracker and sees the crumbs on the seat and smiles.

She takes out her phone and sees Parker has sent her a text.

—*Hey, you must be home by now?*—

—*Yep, just got here. Thank you so much for the beautiful roses and card.*—

—*You're welcome. I hope it wasn't too forward. I just really like you. How was your trip?*—

—*Cold and dark. I miss the Bahamas, and I miss you. And no, your card wasn't too forward.*—

—*I miss you more.*—

Amy sends a smiley face.

—*I'm exhausted. Want to FaceTime tomorrow?*—

—*Absolutely. Sweet dreams, baby.*—

—*You too.*—

She texts her sister, as promised.

—*I'm home safe and sound. I love you.*—

—*I love you too. I'll call you tomorrow night so we can catch up.*—

Amy leaves her plate on the couch and drags herself to bed. Snuggling into the covers, she hugs the body pillow, imagining it's Parker.

She falls asleep and dreams of roses, sweet kisses from Parker, and the hope of new beginnings.

Epilogue

Parker paces the hotel balcony and wipes perspiration from his upper lip. Sweating is constant in Dubai, and he hasn't gotten used to it despite working here for the last two months. The heat from the Arabian Desert is like sticking his head in an oven.

He sits on one of the cherry-red wicker chairs and drums his fingers on the black steel dining table that reflects the blistering sun. It's a sharp contrast to the aqua-green background of the Persian Gulf. His other hand, stuck deep in his pants pocket, plays with the soft velvet box.

He checks his watch. Again. Amy's flight from Egypt lands in an hour. He wills the immigration line to be short and traffic to be light.

I can't wait to feel her body next to mine.

His elevator install was postponed, so he could get to know her better in a few fleeting months—the massive mountain cabin in Washington, her university town, barhopping in Nashville, just outside of his hometown, live music spilling from every venue. Her bright, wide eyes and the way she swayed to the beat. She was sexy as hell.

Unable to sit, he moves into the hotel room. He wanders back outside. He peers over the edge. People on the street below bustle to get somewhere. The low hum rising to his balcony causes a ripple in his stomach—through his travels, he's been to hundreds of cities but prefers his small Southern town. In his hometown, everyone smiles, waves, and makes polite conversation. In Dubai, it's a mass of nameless faces who don't make eye contact. He studies the rush of anonymous folks below, arms full of shopping bags. Luxury cars line the road, yet the seeping wealth doesn't stop them from being impatient and laying on their horns in traffic. Somehow, he'd thought rich folks would be gentler, more patient. But they're not. Not like at home. Home. Amy is home. No matter where they are. He looks at his watch again. *Soon.* Soon she'll be here.

Tired of watching the people, he wanders back inside, pulls the box from his pants pocket, and places it on the coffee table. He plops down on the overstuffed couch and stares at the dark velvet, a sharp contrast to the white marbled table. Parker opens the lid, closes it, opens it yet again, and checks his phone.

Only ten minutes have passed.

Thoughts of Amy and his daughter, Olivia, dance in his head. Their first meeting was like a perfect dream, which sealed the deal with Amy, and led to the box he can't stop gawking at, a box that will change his life. She was ideal for him, but what about Olivia? She didn't have kids, so he had no idea how she'd handle a four-year-old. He had an answer in less than fifteen minutes.

They had walked through Gaylord Opryland Resort just after picking Amy up from the airport. Olivia grabbed Amy's hand. Amy leaned down and whispered in Olivia's ear, and they smiled at each other. Amy pointed out the waterfalls in the giant atrium to Olivia.

He'd overheard her telling his daughter about the waterfalls just outside of her hometown in the mountains, and Olivia's eyes widened, wanting to hear more. She'd asked Amy, "Can I come and see them?"

Amy didn't miss a beat. "Of course! I'd love to have you."

As they'd made their way toward the restaurant, Olivia asked, "Swing me, Daddy. Amy." His daughter stood in the middle and took both of their hands. He glanced at Amy to try and explain what Olivia meant, but Amy wasn't looking at him. She was gazing at his little girl, her beautiful blue eyes crinkling at the edges. "Ready?"

They swung Olivia up and down as they walked past shops. Replicas of miniature houses. She giggled.

Amy gets it.

I need to make her mine, ours, he had thought, wetness creeping into the corners of his eyes. When Amy went to the ladies' room, Olivia leaned over, serious, and asked, "Do you love her? If so, you should marry her. That's what my teacher says people do when they're in love. I hope you do love her, Daddy. I like her, and she makes you smile. Like, all the time."

He was taken aback at how grown-up she sounded. He fumbled for words and then leaned in and whispered, "Yes, I do love her, and I would like to marry her. I'm glad you like her. But let's keep the marrying thing to ourselves for now, okay?"

Olivia had put her hand to her mouth, as if to zip it up, showing him her lips were sealed. He laughed and looked away to wipe his eyes.

Parker wiggles on the plush couch as he notices the room as if for the first time. Stark modern furniture and the black steel counters and appliances in the kitchen create reflections that dance on the ceiling. And who knew hotel rooms had kitchens; he didn't, despite the fact he's spent his entire career in hotel rooms. He hopes Amy loves this suite. *She'll say yes. I'm sure of it.*

Unable to take his gaze off the box, he texts his best friend, Zach. —*I'm worried Amy won't say yes that she won't be happy in Nashville, with...me.*—

—*Quit being a pussy.*— Zach tells him. —*Just do the deed.*—

Zach and his wife sound like they still have some shit to figure out. Parker makes a mental note to touch base with Zach on the phone tomorrow. Parker takes a shower, shaves, and pats his neck with cologne. Dressed, he glances at himself in the mirror. Amy had once told him he looked hot in the short-sleeve polo shirt he's wearing. He shoves down the anxious nausea.

He sits back down and opens the box. Light from the crystal chandelier hits the platinum band and emerald-cut diamond, casting rainbows on the ceiling. He puts the ring on his pinky finger and twists it around. He returns it to the case and shoves it in his pocket. *Six-months' salary for an engagement ring. Damn. That is a lot of fucking money. She's worth it.*

He reaches up and gives his neck a quick rub. He shakes his head as there's a soft knock at the door. His stomach drops. *She's here already?* He moves to the door and opens it. *No, it's the chef. Right on time.*

The chef had suggested fish and some kind of fancy souffle for dinner and raised an eyebrow when Parker told him no. "I want French fries and mozzarella sticks for appetizers, steak and baked potato for the main course, and chocolate cake for dessert." Amy's favorite foods. When the chef had huffed, Parker gazed at him until the man looked away.

The chef unloads boxes. Parker realizes he's staring. He grabs the velvet box from the coffee table, slips it into his pants pocket, and continues to rub his fingers over it. *Jesus, there isn't going to be any velvet left if I keep this up.*

Another knock at the door startles him.

He opens the door and can't see a face through the dozens of red roses. *The florist.*

"Where would you like me to put the flowers?"

"On the coffee table, thank you."

Parker works on the roses, a needed distraction from his nerves. He takes one bouquet and sets it on the balcony table where they'll have dinner. He plucks the petals from the flowers and scatters them on the platform bed, and in the enormous bathroom jetted tub, throughout the hallways, and at the front door. The chef barely notices, only glancing up for a second to give him a sympathetic grin.

Parker steps back and takes in the room. *I did good.*

His phone beeps. *Amy?* His heart drops when he sees it's his new friend, Jaden, from the Bahamas. He's texting to confirm plans to visit Nashville this summer.

Just as Parker finishes the text, another one comes through. *It's her.* He pats down the chub forming in his pants at the thought of seeing her naked, as his fiancée, in just a few short hours. His dick is relentless, just as much, maybe more, as the first time he saw her walking through the hotel lobby in the Bahamas.

She's landed. She found the car he'd sent for her.

—I'm on my way. I feel like a princess or famous actress. The car is so fancy.—

He can't help but laugh as he texts back. *—Only the best for you, babe.—*

He grips the box in his pocket, then stops. He's being ridiculous. Moving toward the kitchen, he confirms with the chef when he wants appetizers served and then heads down to the lobby to wait for her.

Parker stands at the curb and shifts his weight from one leg to the other. He tries not to peer in the back seat of every limousine that passes. Finally, a limo slows down, stops, and she steps out of the open door.

Fuck, she's gorgeous and sexy. He imagines her long hair brushing his chest and inner thighs later.

He rushes to her, and when she turns around, she smiles wide. He pulls her into his arms. When they pull apart, he presses his mouth on hers. Her lips taste like the peppermint-red lipstick she always wears.

"Baby. I'm so happy to see you," she gushes.

"Me too. I sure missed you."

She twists the straps of the crossbody bag he surprised her with in the Bahamas around her fingers and gazes at him naughtily, her blue eyes sparkling. *Fuck.* He adjusts his pants. Parker gathers her luggage from the driver, pays him, and they make their way to the room, talking about the flight.

She saunters into the room and gasps.

"Oh my God, Parker, this is beautiful!" She leaps when she sees the chef who pretends not to see them.

"That's our private chef for the evening."

"Oh wow. Hi." She moves in small circles, taking in the room. "This is gorgeous."

He takes her luggage into the bedroom, and she

kicks her shoes off and hops onto the bed, laughing. She jumps high, her feet nearly touching her ass. "This is the best room I've ever been in."

He steps up, glad that she's taught him this routine, clasps her hands, and they jump together, circling and jumping as high as they can. He glances through the doorway at the chef, who grins, face flushed when their gaze meets, and then looks away. They fall onto the plush purple comforter together, laughing.

On the balcony, he pours them both a glass of Malbec. She tells him about swimming with pink dolphins in the Nile, and Lexi's antics on their trip to Egypt.

"Lexi really liked our tour guide. I've never seen her so enamored. I sure hope it works out for her."

Parker recalls meeting Lexi—she'd driven the two hours from Spokane to Amy's to meet him a couple of months ago. During dinner, she'd flirted with the server and talked a million miles a minute. She was overwhelming. But Amy loves her, therefore, so do I.

"I'm so glad you could swing through here on your way home."

"Me too. Honestly, though, I can't believe we're here together in Dubai. Only three more months till my big move to Nashville. It's hard to imagine. It's all happened so fast, but somehow it doesn't seem that quick, you know?" Amy bites her lip.

"Yeah, Zach told me at first he thought we were moving too swift until he saw us together."

"Ha. My friends said the same thing." She takes a large sip of the wine, her teeth already stained red. *Cute.*

"And to think, you were just going to make me a

vacation fling. You know, giving me the wrong number and all." Parker smiles wickedly at her.

"You knew about that?"

"Yep." They smirk at each other. He tries to shove the butterflies down in his stomach.

They discuss the details of her upcoming move to Nashville, her great new job as chair of the Communications Department, about Olivia, and Parker's friends.

"Appetizers are served," the chef interrupts, setting down plates of food.

Parker wiggles in his chair. *When should I ask?*

Amy looks at the plate of mozzarella sticks and French fries, and her eyes widen. "You're fucking kidding me? Two of my favorite foods. You're the best." She gets out of her chair, hugs him, and sits on his lap and kisses him.

He doesn't want it to end. Reluctantly he lets her go.

When she moves back to her seat, he adjusts his pants to accommodate for his growing dick. Again. *Her ass... Calm down and just do it.*

He pulls the box out of his pocket and palms it in his hand.

"Amy Russo."

Her eyes widen, and she swallows hard. He kneels in front of her.

"I never want to be without you. I hope this will be the first day of our rose-filled future together. Will you marry me?" He pulls the box from his pocket.

Her mouth falls open, and she holds her hands to her cheeks. Tears appear in the corners of her eyes.

"Fuck yes!"

He slips the ring out of the box and puts it on her finger.

"It's beautiful. We are beautiful together, so a hundred times yes!" A tear rolls down her cheek.

He stands and pulls her out of her chair, wrapping her in his arms. Now, they'll never really have to say goodbye. Amy's engagement ring glows in the moonlight over Dubai.

Parker glances at the sky, with her in his arms, and thanks whatever karma was at play when she walked through that lobby in the Bahamas. That was the second-best day of his romantic life. Today is the first.

About the Author

Lola is a university professor by day and a naughty writer and reader by night. For fun, Lola loves camping, boating, playing with her two black labs, and of course, writing anything fun and sexy.

~*~

Visit Lola at

www.lolavalet.com

Also Available
from The Wild Rose Press, Inc.
and major retailers.

Amber Eyes
In Their Eyes Book One
By Gabbi Black

School principal Gage Clayton is still grieving the death of his wife and submissive, yet he can't ignore his Dominant needs. As he enters Club Kink, he's inexplicably drawn to a newly released sub with an intriguing proposition and the most captivating amber eyes. But she has disturbing baggage and her expectations prove quite a challenge, one that would necessitate a commitment he's not ready for.

Rielle Reid needs a Dom while she waits for her former Master to return. When she invites a handsome stranger to her home dungeon for a night of play, she's surprised at his gentle dominance—and her response to it. But in the light of day, his demand for equal footing confounds her. After living four years as a twenty-four/seven slave, she has no concept of how to be anything other than property.

Gage must find a way to master Rielle to free them both from the shackles of the past.

Also Available
from The Wild Rose Press, Inc.
and major retailers.

Angel's Collar
Love Strictly Tested Book One
By Anna Hague

I have it all…until he shows me more.

I didn't intentionally spill wine all over the most beautiful guy in the room, and one look at those icy-blue eyes brings on a major lapse in coherent speech. Jordan Caldera tells me his secret and wants me to join him. This is where my journey into submission begins.

So much about BDSM freaks me out, but at the same time, I can't help but be intrigued. When I imagine Jordan doing those things to me, I can't resist the adventure. Mind-blowing sex aside, my life is changing at an alarming rate and getting very complicated. Between balancing my career and my best friend's concerns, the secrets I'm keeping are killing me.

What am I willing to risk for the new lifestyle I've embraced…and the man I love?

Thank you for purchasing
this publication of The Wild Rose Press, Inc.

For questions or more
information contact us at
info@thewildrosepress.com.

The Wild Rose Press, Inc.
www.thewildrosepress.com